THE THREE LEMONS
&
OTHER STORIES

Publications from
The Scheherazade Foundation

The Secrets of Scheherazade
An Ordered Experience
Tale of a Lantern & Other Stories
The Elephant & The Tortoise & Other Stories
The Monkey's Fiddle & Other Stories
Ghost of the Violet Well & Other Stories
Many Wise Fools & Other Stories
The Frog Prince & Other Stories
The Three Lemons & Other Stories
The Twelve-Headed Griffin & Other Stories
The Antelope Boy & Other Stories
Why the Fish Laughed & Other Stories
Two Cats & Other Stories
Three Stories
The Twilight of the Gods & Other Stories
The Son of Seven Queens & Other Stories
The Moon Maiden & Other Stories
The Metamorphosis & Other Stories
The Celestial Sisters & Other Stories
Tales from the Arabian Nights I
East of the Sun, West of the Moon & Other Stories
The Well at the End of the World & Other Stories

THE THREE LEMONS
&
OTHER STORIES

Edited & Introduced by

TAHIR SHAH

The Scheherazade Foundation

The Scheherazade Foundation CIC
85 Great Portland Street
London
W1W 7LT
United Kingdom
www.SF.Charity
info@SF.Charity

First published by The Scheherazade Foundation CIC, 2023

THE THREE LEMONS
&
OTHER STORIES

The Three Lemons
Folk Tales from Many Lands
Lilian Gask
T.Y. Crowell & Co.
1910

The Physician's Son & the King of the
Snakes
Zanzibar Tales
George W. Bateman
A.C. McClurg & Co.
1901

The King & the Apple
Georgian Folk Tales
Marjory Wardrop
David Nutt Ltd.
1894

The Flying Lion
Outa Karel's Stories
Sanni Metelerkamp
Macmillan & Co.
1914

Godmother Death
*Sixty Folk-Tales from Exclusively
Slavonic Sources*
A. H. Wratislaw
Elliot Stock
1889

The Weeoonibeens & the Piggiebillah
Australian Legendary Tales
David Nutt Ltd.
1896

The Runaways
*Wigwam Evenings: Sioux Folk Tales
Retold*
Charles Alexander Eastman & Elaine
Goodale Eastman
Little, Brown & Co.
1909

Käthchen & the Kobold
Fairy Tales from the German Forests
Margaret Arndt
Everett & Co. Ltd.
1913

The Husband Who Was to Mind the
House
East of the Sun & West of the Moon
Peter Christen Asbjørnsen & Jørgen
Engebretsen Moe
George H. Doran Co.
1924

The Eagles
Polish Fairy Tales
A. J. Glinski
John Lane Co.
1920

About Bears: By One of Them
The Romance of the Woods
F. J. Whishaw
Longmans, Green & Co.
1895

The Great Flood
The Chinese Fairy Book
Dr R. Wilhelm
Frederick A. Stokes Co.
1921

ISBN 978-1-915311-09-2

CONTENTS

Series Introduction		1
The Three Lemons	Turkey	7
The Physician's Son &		
the King of the Snakes	Zanzibar	19
The King & the Apple	Georgia	34
The Flying Lion	South Africa	38
Godmother Death	Czech Republic	44
The Weeoonibeens &		
the Piggiebillah	Australia	49
The Runaways	USA	54
Käthchen & the Kobold	Germany	58
The Husband Who Was to		
Mind the House	Norway	75
The Eagles	Poland	78
About Bears: By One of Them	Russia	85
The Great Flood	China	121

Series Introduction

FROM EARLIEST CHILDHOOD, I was told stories.

Of course I was – most children are told stories.

After all, telling children stories is one of the foundations that makes their early experiences a childhood.

But as I think back to the first years of my own life, I find myself reeling from the sheer quantity of stories my infant ears took in.

Whereas other children my age were told stories for amusement, my parents (and the people they associated with) recounted the endless streams of tales for a different reason.

In their opinion, stories – and the ability to tell them – were part of an ancient alchemy... a way of processing complex ideas, of solving problems, and of developing the human mind.

My father, the writer and thinker Idries Shah, believed that folklore was the single most important breakthrough ever developed by the human species. The way he saw it, the rise of stories was as consequential as the development of the languages in which they were told.

He would say that, without stories and storytelling, humanity would never have evolved in the way that it has – and that the folktales, which form a bedrock of ancient societies, are more precious than any physical artefact unearthed on an archaeological dig.

As the years of my own childhood slipped by, I found myself unbothered to work out the hidden layers within treasuries of stories – what my father called 'instruction manuals to the world'. Like everyone else, I simply absorbed the individual tales, delighting in them.

And that's it – the key point, the genius of stories and storytelling.

It's a thing I only grasped in adulthood… something that fascinates me deeply.

In the same way you can jump into a car and drive across the country without giving a second thought to the engine or how it works, you can appreciate stories without understanding the hidden layers and devices that make them what they are.

Stories are all around us.

They're in the TV and movies we so adore, in the video games we play, and of course in the books we read. They're in newspapers and magazines, too; in the conversations we share with old friends, and with new ones. They're on our mobile phones, in aeroplanes, in submarines, and even in our dreams.

Our obsession with, and craving for, stories rests squarely with the way we are so absorbed by them, just as it does with the way we don't need to continually consider how and why they work.

Throughout my life, I've devoted an increasing amount of time to gathering stories from all corners of the world.

It began in my late teens, when I began to criss-cross the continents in a crazed preoccupation with folklore. I developed a first-hand love affair with societies that, over millennia, gave birth to their own astonishing traditions of stories and storytelling.

Most of the time, when reading or listening to stories, we forget that these tales have been shaped through the passage of time. Like pebbles in a river smoothed by rushing waters, they were honed through centuries of telling and retelling.

When I was twelve years old, my father published a masterwork, *World Tales*. The first edition was very large and featured hundreds of original illustrations. The book was unlike any that had come before, for it detailed the provenance and history of each story told.

At bedtime one night, he presented me with an advanced copy. For as long as I could remember, my father had been talking about the project.

Having an actual copy in my hands at last was thrilling beyond words.

Peering down at me sternly, my father said:

'This is far more than a book, Tahir Jan. It's the foundation stone of a great building… a building that *is* human culture. As you grow older, and as you go out into the world, you will understand that the folklores contained between the covers of *World Tales* have brought amusement and educated, and have solved problems when they were needed most of all.'

My father was right.

When I eventually headed out into the wilds of the world for the first time, I discovered the stories contained in *World Tales* for myself, along with a great many more. Just as he said, the stories published in his treasury were the warp and weft threads of society. Stories are the matrix on which culture itself is based – a framework that enables daily life to continue as smoothly as it does.

In this series of books, we have drawn together stories from all over the world. It's a mission begun decades ago by *World Tales*.

Some of the pieces will be known to you, and others will not.

Some will be easy to comprehend, while others will be challenging, or even nonsensical.

I'd now like to note something else...

The Occidental world seems to assume stories must appear in certain regimented ways – presented with a well-defined beginning, a middle, and an end. You know what I mean: the protagonist winning against all odds, and the happy ending to it all.

In the ancient tradition of teaching stories, the kind recounted for an eternity around campfires in the desert and in longhouses deep in the jungle, there's no such standardisation.

Rather, there's usually a hotchpotch of conflicting threads: stories without a straight linear narrative but with an underlying turbulence that gets the reader, or the listener, to sit up and think.

At The Scheherazade Foundation, we are preoccupied with the way we can extract knowledge from stories – either deliberately, or in a less structured way.

We hold the firm opinion that, in order to remove the marrow from the bone stories are best served up in the way as they were passed from one generation to the next throughout human history.

In this series, we have drawn together tales that were gathered in particular during the nineteenth and early twentieth centuries. Spanning a vast range of cultures, they offer an extraordinary glimpse into the societies from which they are drawn – societies that were often changed shortly afterwards by social upheaval, technologies, and war.

Indeed, the fact any of them were recorded at all is a thing of wonder.

Intriguingly, some of the tales will now appear dated because vocabulary and writing styles have altered. But the fact that they seem old-fashioned is of great interest – proof of the way stories are constantly changing and evolving from one era to the next.

Over the last thirty years, I've gathered hundreds of tales on my own journeys, most of them spoken directly into my ears by storytellers and fellow travellers, by wizened old men in the middle of nowhere, and by anyone else good enough to indulge my pleas.

On all those zigzagging adventures, one story sticks out, tantalising me whenever I turn it around my head.

It was called 'The Man Who Turned into a Cat'.

The reason I mention it here is not because it was an especially fine tale, but rather because, from that moment, it affected the way I perceive the world.

It was as though I were a lock and that, by hearing the tale, a key had been slipped into me and turned.

Since first receiving it, I've never been quite the same, my state of consciousness having been flipped inside out.

The fellow traveller who recounted 'The Man Who Turned into a Cat' was lost in shadow, no more than a fragment of his left cheek protruding shyly into the light.

We were sitting on low divans in a teahouse in the ancient Afghan city of Herat.

When the tale had been whispered, I sat there in silence for a long while.

'What have you done to me?' I asked after a long pause.

The fellow traveller offered half a smile.

'*I* didn't do anything,' he replied. 'It's the story that's affected you – a story that I myself first heard when I was a child playing in the orchards of Balkh.'

Peering into the shadow, my eyes widened.

'I don't understand,' I said feebly. 'After all, it's not an especially grand story. There wasn't even a jinn.'

The traveller's mouth eased out from the shadows.

Very slowly, it grinned.

'Tales containing the greatest sustenance for a soul speak in the softest voice,' he said.

Tahir Shah

The Three Lemons

A CERTAIN SULTAN had a son of whom he was justly proud, for the young man was handsome and gay of temper, and had never been known to do an unworthy action.

In the circle of the court he was the brightest star, and very sweet were the glances thrown him by the high-born ladies who served the Sultan. The prince was courteous to them all, but he favoured no one, and as years went on, and he showed no signs of taking to himself a wife, the Sultan became disturbed.

'My son,' he said, 'why do you not choose a bride? It is time you were married, for I should like to see you the father of children before I go to my rest. Surely it would be easy to find a mate amidst these fair women you see around you? I should experience no difficulty were I in your place.'

The young prince looked at him thoughtfully.

'I must have something more than any of them can give me, my father,' he replied, 'and if you really wish me to take a wife, I will go on a long journey, perhaps even round the world, and seek a princess whom I can love. She must be fair as the morning, white as the snow, and as pure as an angel.'

'Well said, my son,' replied the Sultan.

'I wish you good fortune and a safe return.' And without more ado the prince departed.

The air was crisp with frost, and the glittering crystals of the snow threw back the radiance of the sunlight from bank to meadow. The waves that tossed and tumbled on the distant shore seemed to beckon him towards them, so he hastened to the coast, where he found a splendid vessel resting at anchor. While he was yet wondering how it had come there, and whither it was bound, invisible hands drew him on board, and, as his feet touched the deck, the anchor lifted, and the ship set sail.

For three days and three nights it glided swiftly over the sea, steered by a shadowy pilot who spoke no word. On the morning of the fourth day it came to a stop beside a little islet, and the prince was amazed to see his favourite horse issue from the hold, ready saddled and bridled. Concluding that he was expected to land, he led the horse on shore, and when he turned round to take another look at the ship, it had completely vanished.

No sign of any habitation was to be seen, and the cold was so intense that he could scarcely hold the reins. In spite of this, he rode on and on, till at last he reached a small white house that stood by itself on the top of a hill, unsheltered from the wind. He knocked at the door with eager haste, hoping for the glimpse of a fire, and perhaps some food. His summons was answered by a venerable man on horseback talking to a woman with scanty hair like wisps of snow, who stared at him inquiringly.

'I seek a wife, good mother,' said the prince. 'She must be the most beautiful princess in the world, and as good as she is beautiful. Can you tell me where to find her? '

The old woman half shut the door.

'You will not find her here,' she said, 'for I am Winter, and this is my kingdom. My sister Autumn perhaps may help you, but I have no time for thoughts of love. You will find her if you go straight on.'

The prince thanked the old lady, and remounted his horse, hoping that Autumn would at least give him rest and refreshment. After a while he found that the snow had disappeared, and that luscious fruit now hung in clusters from the trees. The stubble of the corn tinted the fields with gold, and the squirrels were busily engaged in storing nuts for the winter. A little further on he came to a small brown house beside a wood, and, again dismounting, he knocked at the door. It was opened by a woman with abundant dark hair and eyes like berries. Her cheeks were ruddy, and her look was kind; she did not, however, ask him in.

'What are you seeking, young man?' she inquired in a gentle voice.

'I seek a wife,' he answered briefly.

'Ah,' she exclaimed, 'then I cannot help you. My name is Autumn, and I am far too busy gathering fruit to have time to spare for such things as love and marriage. My sister Summer is full of dreams, and she may find you what you want.'

So saying, she shut the door, and as there was nothing else for him to do, the prince resumed his journey.

He noticed ere long that the grass by the roadside was very tall, and that the fields were heavy with corn ready for harvest. The air was so warm that it touched his cheek caressingly, and the sun shone down so hotly that he was fain to unloose his coat. He was very glad when at last he saw a small yellow house shaded by a group of trees. As he knocked at the door, he heard the sound of a distant waterfall, and the hope of quenching his thirst was more in his mind just then than the fairest wife in Summer's kingdom. His summons was answered by a stately woman crowned with auburn tresses.

'I am sorry I cannot help you,' she said, when he had told her the object of his journey, 'for I, too, am very busy. Hasten you to my sister Spring; she is the friend of lovers, and will surely aid you.'

So the prince went on till he saw a little green house in a bower of lilac. Hyacinths and violets, jonquils, narcissi, and fragrant lilies-of-the-valley grew beneath the windows, and, when he knocked at the door, a little lady with flaxen hair, and eyes of soft deep violet, appeared on the threshold.

'Won't you take pity on me?' he asked her eagerly. 'Your sisters sent me on to you. I seek a wife, who must be fair as the morning, white as the snow, and pure as an angel from Heaven.'

'You ask a great deal,' Spring told him, smilingly, 'but I will do my best for you. Come in and rest – you must be tired and hungry.'

And to his great delight she ushered him into a long, low room, filled with the scent of flowers.

When he had feasted on bread and honey, and quenched his thirst with sweet new milk, she brought him three fine lemons on a crystal tray. Beside them was a handsome silver knife, and a quaint gold cup of rare design.

'These are magic gifts,' she said, 'so guard them carefully. Return at once to your own home, and make your way to the great fountains in the palace gardens. Having made quite sure that you are alone, take your silver knife and cut open the first lemon. As you do so, a lovely princess will instantly appear, and will ask you to give her water. If you at once offer her some in this golden cup, she will stay with you and be your wife, but should you hesitate, even for the space of a second, she will vanish into thin air, and you will never see her again.'

'I am not likely to be so foolish,' said the prince, 'but if I do, shall I have no wife at all?'

'You must then cut open the second lemon,' Spring answered gravely, 'and exactly the same thing will occur. If you hesitate this time also, and she too disappears, you will have one more chance with the third lemon. Should your wits fail you a third time, you will die without a mate.'

The prince would have thanked her for her kindness, but she waved him away with a smile and a sigh, telling him not to delay. Full of joyful anticipation, he rode once more through the kingdoms of Summer, Autumn, and Winter, and when he arrived at the coast found the same stately vessel awaiting his pleasure. The wind was favourable on his homeward voyage, and in a very short time he had once more gained the precincts of his father's palace. Giving his horse into the care of a groom, he hurried into the great gardens, and, when he had filled Spring's gold cup with water from the splashing fountains, cut open the first lemon. He had no sooner done so, than a most exquisite princess appeared before him, and with a timid glance asked him to give her water.

'I am thirsty,' she murmured. 'Will you not let me drink from your golden cup?'

The prince was so lost in admiration that he could only gaze at her, and with a gesture of reproach the lovely maiden vanished. It was in vain that he lamented his stupidity. Do as he would, he could not call her back again, and with many regrets he cut the rind of the second lemon. Once more the gleaming spray of the dancing fountains took the form of a beautiful girl.

'Fair as the morning and white as snow!' cried the prince in rapture, too delighted to heed her request for a cup of water. He did not regain his senses until she also had disappeared, when he again bewailed his neglect of Spring's injunctions. With trembling fingers, he inserted the silver knife into the third lemon, and as the pungent odour of the golden fruit escaped into the air another princess appeared before him. Closing his eyes, lest they might be dazzled by her exceeding beauty, he immediately offered the golden cup. The maiden raised it to her lips with a bewitching smile, and drained it to its dregs. The prince laughed aloud for joy; now at last he had found the bride he sought.

No summer morning was fairer than she, for the whiteness of snow gleamed on chin and brow, and her expression was pure and gentle as an angel's. Drawing her down beside him on to a flowery bank, he held her hand and looked into her eyes.

'Will you be my wife?' he whispered, and to his delight she answered,

'Yes.'

When his first raptures were over, he noticed, with some disappointment, the simplicity of his bride's gown. It was of some simple stuff the colour of running water, and hung in long flowing folds round her lissom form. No necklace broke the outline of her dainty throat, and she looked so different from the maidens of the court that the prince, who, after all, was only a man, and not, perhaps, a very wise one, felt that something was lacking to complete her beauty.

'Your robe is not worthy of you, dear love,' he cried. 'If you wait for me here, I will fetch you one of rich white satin from my father's palace, and a rope of pearls to twine around your neck.'

But the princess knew that she needed no ornaments to enhance her beauty, and she did not wish him to leave her. Her lover, however, was so insistent that she consented to stay by the fountains while he went home, and, more in love with her than ever, he hurried away.

Now the princess was very timid, and as the prince tarried long she grew frightened of being alone. So she stretched out her arms to a tree above her, and swung herself up that she might nestle amidst its branches. The foliage hid her slender limbs in their flowing draperies, but her exquisite face gleamed like a flower from a setting of glossy leaves, and was mirrored in the deep basin of the fountains. A plain handmaid who came to fill her pitcher caught sight of its loveliness, and, since she had never gazed into a mirror, believed it to be her own.

'Oh, how very handsome I am!' she murmured. 'I am far too beautiful to do the bidding of any mistress. I will never draw water again.'

And flinging the pitcher from her, she strutted home with the air of a peacock.

'Why have you come back empty-handed, Deborah?' inquired her mistress.

'I have seen my face in the fountain,' was the reply, 'and I am much too lovely to fetch and carry like a poor slave.'

'Why, you are as plain as day!' her mistress retorted sharply. 'Go back at once, and do as you are told.'

Deborah fetched another pitcher and went back to the fountains, grumbling the while. Again she caught sight of the princess's face reflected in the water, and again her swarthy features became distorted with pride.

'It is true!' she cried. 'I am lovely as a dream. I will marry a prince, and live in a palace.'

With this she threw down the second pitcher, and flounced into her mistress's presence with such an assumption of dignity that that lady burst out laughing.

'If you only knew how plain you are,' she cried, when she could speak, 'you would never talk such ridiculous nonsense.'

And daring her to return again without the water, she handed the mortified woman a third pitcher and sent her back to the fountain.

The flower-like face of the fair princess smiled back at the plain maid as she bent over the pool, and the poor creature grinned and ogled.

'But I am handsome,' she cried triumphantly. 'As handsome as a queen.'

She spoke so loudly that the princess heard her, and her laugh rang out like a peal of bells. Looking hastily up, the handmaid saw her in the branches, and disappointed vanity rendered her almost speechless... Her mistress was right then, after all, and the lovely vision she had seen in the water was not the reflection of herself. As she stared upward with dilated eyes, there came to her thoughts of revenge.

'I will make her suffer for this,' she murmured, but wreathing her wide lips in a false smile, she bade the princess: 'Good morrow. Why do you hide in a tree, lovely lady?' she asked her gently.

'I am waiting for my prince, who has gone to fetch me a satin robe, and a rope of pearls to twine round my neck,' answered the princess shyly.

'Your golden hair has been tossed by the wind,' remarked the handmaid.

'Let me come up beside you, and I will make it smooth. It will not do to look untidy when your prince arrives!'

'How kind you are!' said the princess, and as she bent her silken head towards the handmaid, the treacherous woman stabbed it with a long sharp pin.

The princess fell back, faint with pain, but before her body could touch the ground she turned into a snow-white pigeon, and flew off uttering plaintive cries.

The handmaid took her place in the tree, and when at last the prince appeared, bearing a satin robe and a bridal veil, it was she whom he saw looking down on him.

Where is my sweet princess?' he asked. 'She is fair as the morning, and white as snow. What have you done with her?'

'Alas! Dear prince,' answered the handmaid sadly, 'while you were away an enchantress came and changed me into my present form. When you have proved your love by making me your wife, I shall, in three days' time, once more become a fair and beautiful princess; but if you desert me, I must remain for ever hideous.'

Although the sight of her filled him with repulsion, the prince was a man of honour, and would not break his word. Calling the ladies who were waiting in the carriage which he had brought to convey his bride to the palace, he bade them array her in the satin gown, and, pretending not to see their astonishment and disgust, drove back with her to his father, introducing her as his promised wife.

The Sultan was naturally horrified at her appearance, but when the prince explained to him how matters stood, he agreed that he must marry her, and hope for the best.

While the father and son talked thus together, the handmaid wandered over the palace, giving unnecessary orders to the servants, and making herself hateful to all. She even ventured into the great kitchens, and commanded the chief cook to prepare rich viands for her wedding ceremonies. As she issued her orders in a loud, harsh voice, she passed by the window, and noticed a slim white pigeon sitting on the sill.

'Kill me that bird,' she cried, 'and cook it for my supper.'

Not daring to disobey her, the chief cook killed it immediately, plunging a sharp knife into its snowy breast. Three drops of blood fell from the windowsill into the courtyard, and a tiny seedling sprang from each of these. As if a fairy had waved her wand, they grew into trees of fragrant blossom, and in an instant the blossom turned into golden lemons.

Meanwhile the prince was seeking for his bride, for since he had set himself so distasteful a task, he wished to perform it well.

'She is in the kitchen, your Royal Highness,' he was informed by one of his shocked courtiers, and in going to meet her, the prince passed under the lemon-trees. The sight of their fruit brought him a ray of hope, and gathering three of the finest that he could find, he hastened with them to his own room, where, having filled the golden cup with water, he plunged the blade of the silver knife into the rind of the first lemon.

As before, a beautiful girl appeared, and stretched out her fair hands for the golden cup.

'Ah, no!' he cried. 'You are very charming, but you are not my princess.'

He cut the rind of a second lemon, and as he did so the second princess took form before him. He shook his head at her mute entreaty for a cup of water, and she too disappeared. Then he cut the rind of the third lemon, and lo, his own princess was once more in his arms!

Great was the joy and relief of the old Sultan when he heard from the prince that this beautiful girl was his real bride, but he listened with a frown of anger as she told them all that had happened when her lover left her by the fountain. He ordered the handmaid to be immediately brought before him, and, regarding her very sternly, asked her what she would think a fitting punishment for an affront offered to the future wife of his dear son.

'Nothing less than death,' declared the handmaid, 'and death by burning. Let the offender be cast into your Majesty's oven, and the great door shut.'

'Madam, you have passed sentence on yourself,' replied the Sultan dryly, and, shrieking with terror, the handmaid was led away.

But the sweet princess would not let her suffer.

'She is but a poor ignorant woman,' she said, 'and it must be sad to be so ugly. Set her free, I entreat you, and let her go. This is the boon I ask you for my wedding gift.'

The Sultan could not refuse his new daughter's first request, and the prince regarded her fondly.

'I saw you were fair as morning, and white as snow,' he murmured, 'and now I know that you are sweet as an angel.'

And though the years to come brought him trouble and sorrow as well as joy, he was indeed blest. Beloved of all, his princess wielded a gentle sway, and he never saw the fruit of a lemon without sending a grateful thought to Spring for the magic gifts by which he had fared so well.

From: Folk Tales from Many Lands

The Physician's Son & the
King of the Snakes

ONCE THERE WAS a very learned physician, who died leaving his wife with a little baby boy, whom, when he was old enough, she named, according to his father's wish, Hasseeboo Karimedin.

When the boy had been to school, and had learned to read, his mother sent him to a tailor, to learn his trade, but he could not learn it. Then he was sent to a silversmith, but he could not learn his trade either. After that he tried many trades, but could learn none of them.

At last, his mother said, 'Well, stay at home for a while;' and that seemed to suit him.

One day he asked his mother what his father's business had been, and she told him he was a very great physician.

'Where are his books?' he asked.

'Well, it's a long time since I saw them,' replied his mother, 'but I think they are behind there. Look and see.'

So he hunted around a little and at last found them, but they were almost ruined by insects, and he gained little from them.

19

At last, four of the neighbours came to his mother and said,

'Let your boy go along with us and cut wood in the forest.'

It was their business to cut wood, load it on donkeys, and sell it in the town for making fires.

'All right,' said she; 'tomorrow I'll buy him a donkey, and he can start fair with you.'

So the next day Hasseeboo, with his donkey, went off with those four persons, and they worked very hard and made a lot of money that day. This continued for six days, but on the seventh day it rained heavily, and they had to get under the rocks to keep dry.

Now, Hasseeboo sat in a place by himself, and, having nothing else to do, he picked up a stone and began knocking on the ground with it. To his surprise the ground gave forth a hollow sound, and he called to his companions, saying, 'There seems to be a hole under here.'

Upon hearing him knock again, they decided to dig and see what was the cause of the hollow sound; and they had not gone very deep before they broke into a large pit, like a well, which was filled to the top with honey.

They didn't do any firewood chopping after that, but devoted their entire attention to the collection and sale of the honey.

With a view to getting it all out as quickly as possible, they told Hasseeboo to go down into the pit and dip out the honey, while they put it in vessels and took it to town for sale. They worked for three days, making a great deal of money.

At last there was only a little honey left at the very bottom of the pit, and they told the boy to scrape that together while they went to get a rope to haul him out.

But instead of getting the rope, they decided to let him remain in the pit, and divide the money among themselves. So, when he had gathered the remainder of the honey together, and called for the rope, he received no answer; and after he had been alone in the pit for three days he became convinced that his companions had deserted him.

Then those four persons went to his mother and told her that they had become separated in the forest, that they had heard a lion roaring, and that they could find no trace of either her son or his donkey.

His mother, of course, cried very much, and the four neighbours pocketed her son's share of the money.

Hasseeboo passed the time walking about the pit, wondering what the end would be, eating scraps of honey, sleeping a little, and sitting down to think.

While engaged in the last occupation, on the fourth day, he saw a scorpion fall to the ground – a large one, too – and he killed it.

Then suddenly he thought to himself,

'Where did that scorpion come from? There must be a hole somewhere. I'll search, anyhow.'

So he searched around until he saw light through a tiny crack; and he took his knife and scooped and scooped, until he had made a hole big enough to pass through; then he went out, and came upon a place he had never seen before.

Seeing a path, he followed it until he came to a very large house, the door of which was not fastened. So he went inside, and saw golden doors, with golden locks, and keys of pearl, and beautiful chairs inlaid with jewels and precious stones, and in a reception room he saw a couch covered with a splendid spread, upon which he lay down.

Presently he found himself being lifted off the couch and put in a chair, and heard someone saying:

'Do not hurt him; wake him gently,' and on opening his eyes he found himself surrounded by numbers of snakes, one of them wearing beautiful royal colours.

'Hullo!' he cried; 'who are you?'

'I am Sultanee Waaneeoka, king of the snakes, and this is my house. Who are you?'

'I am Hasseeboo Karimedin.'

'Where do you come from?'

'I don't know where I come from, or where I'm going.'

'Well, don't bother yourself just now. Let's eat; I guess you are hungry, and I know I am.'

Then the king gave orders, and some of the other snakes brought the finest fruits, and they ate and drank and conversed.

When the repast was ended, the king desired to hear Hasseeboo's story; so he told him all that had happened, and then asked to hear the story of his host.

'Well,' said the king of the snakes, 'mine is rather a long story, but you shall hear it. A long time ago I left this place, to go and live in the mountains of Al Kaaf, for the change of air. One day I saw a stranger coming along, and I said to him,

"Where are you from?" and he said,

"I am wandering in the wilderness."

"Whose son are you?" I asked.

"My name is Bolookeea. My father was a sultan; and when he died, I opened a small chest, inside of which I found a bag, which contained a small brass box; when I had opened this I found some writing tied up in a woollen cloth, and it was all in praise of a prophet. He was described as such a good and wonderful man, that I longed to see him; but when I made inquiries concerning him, I was told he was not yet born. Then I vowed I would wander until I should see him. So I left our town, and all my property, and I am wandering, but I have not yet seen that prophet."

'Then I said to him, "Where do you expect to find him, if he's not yet born? Perhaps if you had some serpent's water you might keep on living until you find him. But it's of no use talking about that; the serpent's water is too far away."

"'Well," he said, "goodbye. I must wander on.'"

So I bade him farewell, and he went his way.

'Now, when that man had wandered until he reached Egypt, he met another man, who asked him, "Who are you?"

"'I am Bolookeea. Who are you?"

"'My name is Al Faan. Where are you going?"

"'I have left my home, and my property, and I am seeking the prophet."

"'Hm!" said Al Faan; "I can tell you of a better occupation than looking for a man that is not born yet. Let us go and find the king of the snakes and get him to give us a charm medicine; then we will go to King Solomon and get his rings, and we shall be able to make slaves of the jinn and order them to do whatever we wish."

'And Bolookeea said, "I have seen the king of the snakes in the mountain of Al Kaaf."

"'All right," said Al Faan; "let's go."

'Now, Al Faan wanted the ring of Solomon that he might be a great magician and control the jinn and the birds, while all Bolookeea wanted was to see the great prophet.

'As they went along, Al Faan said to Bolookeea, "Let us make a cage and entice the king of the snakes into it; then we will shut the door and carry him off."

"'All right," said Bolookeea.

'So they made a cage, and put therein a cup of milk and a cup of wine, and brought it to Al Kaaf; and I, like a fool, went in, drank up all the wine and became drunk. Then they fastened the door and took me away with them.

'When I came to my senses, I found myself in the cage, and Bolookeea carrying me, and I said, "The sons of Adam are no good. What do you want from me?"

'And they answered, "We want some medicine to put on our feet, so that we may walk upon the water whenever it is necessary in the course of our journey."

"'Well," said I, "go along."

'We went on until we came to a place where there were a great number and variety of trees; and when those trees saw me, they said,

"'I am medicine for this;"

"'I am medicine for that;"

"'I am medicine for the head;"

"'I am medicine for the feet;" and presently one tree said,

"'If anyone puts my medicine upon his feet he can walk on water."

'When I told that to those men they said, "That is what we want;" and they took a great deal of it.

'Then they took me back to the mountain and set me free; and we said goodbye and parted.

'When they left me, they went on their way until they reached the sea, when they put the medicine on their feet and walked over. Thus, they went many days, until they came near to the place of King Solomon, where they waited while Al Faan prepared his medicines.

'When they arrived at King Solomon's place, he was sleeping, and was being watched by jinn, and his hand lay on his chest, with the ring on his finger.

'As Bolookeea drew near, one of the jinn said to him, "Where are you going?"

'And he answered, "I'm here with Al Faan; he's going to take that ring."

'"Go back," said the genie; "keep out of the way. That man is going to die."

'When Al Faan had finished his preparations, he said to Bolookeea, "Wait here for me."

Then he went forward to take the ring, when a great cry arose, and he was thrown by some unseen force a considerable distance.

'Picking himself up, and still believing in the power of his medicines, he approached the ring again, when a strong breath blew upon him, and he was burnt to ashes in a moment.

'While Bolookeea was looking at all this, a voice said, "Go your way; this wretched being is dead."

'So he returned; and when he got to the sea again he put the medicine upon his feet and passed over, and continued to wander for many years.

'One morning he saw a man sitting down, and said, "Good morning," to which the man replied.

'Then Bolookeea asked him, "Who are you?" and he answered: "My name is Jan Shah. Who are you?"

'So Bolookeea told him who he was, and asked him to tell him his history. The man, who was weeping and smiling by turns, insisted upon hearing Bolookeea's story first. After he had heard it he said: "Well, sit down, and I'll tell you my story from beginning to end. My name is Jan Shah, and my father is Tooeeghamus, a great sultan. He used to go every day into the forest to shoot game; so one day I said to him,

'"Father, let me go with you into the forest today;" but he said, "Stay at home. You are better there."

'Then I cried bitterly, and as I was his only child, whom he loved dearly, he couldn't stand my tears, so he said: "Very well; you shall go. Don't cry."

'Thus, we went to the forest, and took many attendants with us; and when we reached the place we ate and drank, and then everyone set out to hunt.

'I and my seven slaves went on until we saw a beautiful gazelle, which we chased as far as the sea without capturing it. When the gazelle took to the water I and four of my slaves took a boat, the other three returning to my father, and we chased that gazelle until we lost sight of the shore, but we caught it and killed it. Just then a great wind began to blow, and we lost our way.

'When the other three slaves came to my father, he asked them, "Where is your master?" and they told him about the gazelle and the boat. Then he cried, "My son is lost! My son is lost!" and returned to the town and mourned for me as one dead.

'After a time, we came to an island, where there were a great many birds. We found fruit and water, we ate and drank, and at night we climbed into a tree and slept till morning.

'Then we rowed to a second island, and, seeing no one around, we gathered fruit, ate and drank, and climbed a tree as before. During the night we heard many savage beasts howling and roaring near us.

'In the morning we got away as soon as possible, and came to a third island. Looking around for food, we saw a tree full of fruit like red-streaked apples; but, as we were about to pick some, we heard a voice say, "Don't touch this tree; it belongs to the king."

'Toward night a number of monkeys came, who seemed much pleased to see us, and they brought us all the fruit we could eat.

'Presently I heard one of them say, "Let us make this man our sultan."

'Then another one said: "What's the use? They'll all run away in the morning."

'But a third one said, "Not if we smash their boat."

'Sure enough, when we started to leave in the morning, our boat was broken in pieces. So there was nothing for it but to stay there and be entertained by the monkeys, who seemed to like us very much.

'One day, while strolling about, I came upon a great stone house, having an inscription on the door, which said, "When any man comes to this island, he will find it difficult to leave, because the monkeys desire to have a man for their king. If he looks for a way to escape, he will think there is none; but there is one outlet, which lies to the north. If you go in that direction you will come to a great plain, which is infested with lions, leopards, and snakes. You must fight all of them; and if you overcome them, you can go forward. You will then come to another great plain, inhabited by ants as big as dogs; their teeth are like those of dogs, and they are very fierce. You must fight these also, and if you overcome them, the rest of the way is clear."

'I consulted with my attendants over this information, and we came to the conclusion that, as we could only die, anyhow, we might as well risk death to gain our freedom.

'As we all had weapons, we set forth; and when we came to the first plain we fought, and two of my slaves were killed. Then we went on to the second plain, fought again; my other two slaves were killed, and I alone escaped.

'After that I wandered on for many days, living on whatever I could find, until at last, I came to a town, where I stayed for some time, looking for employment but finding none.

'One day a man came up to me and said, "Are you looking for work?"

'"I am," said I.

'"Come with me, then," said he; and we went to his house.

'When we got there, he produced a camel's skin, and said, "I shall put you in this skin, and a great bird will carry you to the top of yonder mountain. When he gets you there, he will tear this skin off you. You must then drive him away and push down the precious stones you will find there. When they are all down, I will get you down."

'So, he put me in the skin; the bird carried me to the top of the mountain and was about to eat me, when I jumped up, scared him away, and then pushed down many precious stones. Then I called out to the man to take me down, but he never answered me, and went away.

'I gave myself up for a dead man, but went wandering about, until at last, after passing many days in a great forest, I came to a house, all by itself; the old man who lived in it gave me food and drink, and I was revived.

'I remained there a long time, and that old man loved me as if I were his own son.

'One day he went away, and giving me the keys, told me I could open the door of every room except one which he pointed out to me.

'Of course, when he was gone, this was the first door I opened. I saw a large garden, through which a stream flowed. Just then, three birds came and alighted by the side of the stream. Immediately they changed to three most beautiful women. When they had finished bathing, they put on their clothes, and, as I stood watching them, they changed into birds again and flew away.

'I locked the door, and went away; but my appetite was gone, and I wandered about aimlessly. When the old man came back, he saw there was something wrong with me, and asked me what was the matter. Then I told him I had seen those beautiful maidens, that I loved one of them very much, and that if I could not marry her, I should die.

'The old man told me I could not possibly have my wish. He said the three lovely beings were the daughters of the sultan of the jinn, and that their home was a journey of three years from where we then were.

'I told him I couldn't help that. He must get her for my wife, or I should die. At last, he said, "Well, wait till they come again, then hide yourself and steal the clothes of the one you love so dearly."

'So I waited, and when they came again I stole the clothes of the youngest, whose name was Sayadaatee Shems.

'When they came out of the water, this one could not find her clothes. Then I stepped forward and said, "I have them."

'"Ah," she begged, "give them to me, their owner; I want to go away."

But I said to her, "I love you very much. I want to marry you."

'"I want to go to my father," she replied.

'"You cannot go," said I.

'Then her sisters flew away, and I took her into the house, where the old man married us. He told me not to give her those clothes I had taken, but to hide them; because if she ever got them, she would fly away to her old home. So, I dug a hole in the ground and buried them.

'But one day, when I was away from home, she dug them up and put them on; then, saying to the slave I had given her for an attendant, "When your master returns, tell him I have gone home; if he really loves me he will follow me," she flew away.

'When I came home, they told me this, and I wandered, searching for her, many years. At last, I came to a town where one asked me, "Who are you?" and I answered, "I am Jan Shah."

'"What was your father's name?"

'"Taaeeghamus."

'"Are you the man who married our mistress?"

'"Who is your mistress?"

'"Sayadaatee Shems."

'"I am he!" I cried with delight.

'They took me to their mistress, and she brought me to her father and told him I was her husband; and everybody was happy.

'Then we thought we should like to visit our old home, and her father's jinn carried us there in three days. We stayed there a year and then returned, but in a short time my wife died. Her father tried to comfort me, and wanted me to marry another of his daughters, but I refused to be comforted, and have mourned to this day. That is my story.

'Then Bolookeea went on his way and wandered till he died.'

Next Sultaanee Waaneeoka said to Hasseeboo, 'Now, when you go home you will do me injury.'

Hasseeboo was very indignant at the idea, and said, 'I could not be induced to do you an injury. Pray, send me home.'

'I will send you home,' said the king; 'but I am sure that you will come back and kill me.'

'Why, I dare not be so ungrateful,' exclaimed Hasseeboo. 'I swear I could not hurt you.'

'Well,' said the king of the snakes, 'bear this in mind: when you go home, do not go to bathe where there are many people.'

And he said, 'I will remember.'

So, the king sent him home, and he went to his mother's house, and she was overjoyed to find that he was not dead.

Now, the sultan of the town was very sick; and it was decided that the only thing that could cure him would be to kill the king of the snakes, boil him, and give the soup to the sultan.

For a reason known only to himself, the vizier had placed men at the public baths with this instruction:

'If anyone who comes to bathe here has a mark on his stomach, seize him and bring him to me.'

When Hasseeboo had been home three days he forgot the warning of Sultaanee Waaneeoka, and went to bathe with the other people. All of a sudden, he was seized by some soldiers, and brought before the vizier, who said, 'Take us to the home of the king of the snakes.'

'I don't know where it is,' said Hasseeboo.

'Tie him up,' commanded the vizier.

So, they tied him up and beat him until his back was all raw, and being unable to stand the pain he cried, 'Let up! I will show you the place.'

So he led them to the house of the king of the snakes, who, when he saw him, said, 'Didn't I tell you, you would come back to kill me?'

'How could I help it?' cried Hasseeboo. 'Look at my back!'

'Who has beaten you so dreadfully?' asked the king.

'The vizier.'

'Then there's no hope for me. But you must carry me yourself.'

As they went along, the king said to Hasseeboo, 'When we get to your town I shall be killed and cooked. The first skimming the vizier will offer to you, but don't you drink it; put it in a bottle and keep it. The second skimming you must drink, and you will become a great physician. The third skimming is the medicine that will cure your sultan. When the vizier asks you if you drank that first skimming say, "I did."

'Then produce the bottle containing the first, and say, "This is the second, and it is for you."

'The vizier will take it, and as soon as he drinks it he will die, and both of us will have our revenge.'

Everything happened as the king had said. The vizier died, the sultan recovered, and Hasseeboo was loved by all as a great physician.

The King & the Apple

THERE WAS AND there was not at all (of God's best may it be!), there was a king. When the day of his death was drawing nigh, he called his son to him, and said:

'In the day when you go to hunt in the east, take this coffer, but only open it when you are in dire distress.'

The king died, and was buried in the manner he had wished. The prince fell into a state of grief, and would not go outside the door. At last the ministers of state came to the new king, and proposed to him that he should go out hunting. The king was delighted with the idea, and set out for the chase with his suite.

They went eastwards, and killed a great quantity of game. On their way home, the young monarch saw a tower near the road, and wished to know what was in it. He asked one of his viziers to go and try to find out about it. He obeyed, but first said: 'I hope to return in three days, and if I do not I shall be dead.'

Three days passed, and the vizier did not return. The king sent a second, a third, a fourth, but not one of them came back. Then he rose and went himself. When he arrived, he saw written over the door:

'Enter and you will repent; enter not and you will repent.'

'I must do one or the other,' said the king to himself, 'so I shall go in.'

He opened the door and went in. Behold! There stood twelve men with drawn swords. They took his hand and led him into twelve rooms. When he went into the twelfth, he saw a golden couch, on which was stretched a boy of eight or nine years of age. His eyes were closed, and he did not utter a word. The king was told:

'You may ask him three questions, but if he does not understand and answer all of them, you must lose your head.'

The king became very sad, but at last remembered the coffer his father had given him.

'What greater misfortune can I have than to lose my head?' said he to himself.

He took out the coffer and opened it; from it there fell out an apple, which rolled towards the couch.

'What help can this be to me?' said the king.

But the apple began to speak, and told the following tale to the boy:

'A certain man was travelling with his wife and brother, when night fell, and they had no food. The woman's brother-in-law went into a neighbouring village to buy bread; on the way he met brigands, who robbed him and cut off his head. When his brother did not return, the man went to look for him; he met the same fate. The next day the unhappy woman went to seek them, and there she saw her husband and brother-in-law lying in one place with their heads cut off; around was a pool of blood.

'The woman sat down, tore her hair, and began to weep bitterly.

'At that moment there jumped out a little mouse. It began to lick the blood, but the woman took a stone, threw it at the mouse, and killed it. Then the mouse's mother came out and said:

'"Look at me, I can bring my child back to life, but what can you do for your husband and his brother?"

'She pulled up an herb, applied it to the little mouse, and it was restored to life. Then they both disappeared in their hole. The woman rejoiced greatly when she saw this; she also plucked of the same herb, put the heads on the bodies, and applied it to them. Her husband and brother-in-law both came back to life, but alas! She had put the wrong heads on the bodies. Now, my sage youth! Tell me, which was the woman's husband?' concluded the apple.

'He opened his eyes, and said: 'Certainly it was he who had the right head.'

The king was very glad.

'A joiner, a tailor and a priest were travelling together at one time,' began the apple. 'Night came on when they were in a wood; they lighted a huge fire, had their supper, and then said: "Do not let us be deprived of employment, each of us shall in turn watch, and do something in his trade."

'The joiner's turn came first. He cut down a tree, and out of it he fashioned a man. Then he lay down, and went to sleep, while the tailor mounted guard. When he saw the wooden man, he took off his clothes and put them on it. Last of all, the priest acted as sentinel. When he saw the man, he said: "I will pray to God that He may give this man a soul."

'He prayed, and his wish was granted. Now, my boy, can you tell me who made the man?'

'He who gave him the soul.'

The king was pleased and said to himself: 'That is two.'

The apple again went on: 'There were a diviner, a physician, and a swift runner.

'The diviner said: "There is a certain prince who is ill with such and such a disease."

'The physician said: "I know a cure for it."

'"I will run with it," said the swift runner.

'The physician prepared the medicine, and the man ran with it. Now tell me who cured the king's son?' said the apple.

'He who made the medicine,' replied the boy.

When he had given the three answers, the apple rolled back into the casket, and the king put it in his pocket. The boy arose, embraced the king, and kissed him: 'Many men have been here, but I have not been able to speak before: now tell me what you wish, and I will do it.'

The king asked that his viziers might be restored to life, and they all went away with rich presents.

From: Georgian Folk Tales

The Flying Lion

'ONCE UPON A time,' remarked Grandpa, thoughtfully, 'Uncle Lion used to fly.'

'O-o-o-oh!' said the children all together, and their eyes widened with terror at the picture called up by Grandpa's words.

'Yes, my master, and then nothing could live before him. His wings were not covered with feathers: they were like the wings of Brother Bat, all skin and ribs; but they were very big, and very thick, and very strong, and when he wasn't flying, they were folded flat against his sides. When he was angry, he let the points down to the ground – tr-r-r-r – like Mister Turkey when he gobble-gobble-gobbles and struts before his wives – tr-r-r-r, and when he wanted to rise from the ground he spread them out and flapped them up and down slowly at first – so, my master; then faster and faster – so, so, so – till he made a big wind with them and sailed away into the air.'

Outa, flapping his crooked arms and puffing out his disproportionate chest, seemed about to follow suit, but suddenly subsided again on to his stool.

'Ach, but it was a terrible sight! Then, when he was high above the earth, he would look down for something to kill.

If he saw a herd of springbuck, he would fly along till he was just over them and pick out a nice fat one; then he would stretch out his iron claws, fold his wings and – whoops! – down he would fall on the poor antelope before it had time to jump away. Yes, that was the way Uncle Lion hunted in the olden times.

'There was only one thing he was afraid of, and that was that the bones of the animals he caught and ate would be broken to pieces. No one knew why, and everyone was too frightened of Uncle Lion to try and find out. He used to keep them all at his home in the cliffs, and he had crows to look after them, two at a time – not like the ugly black crows that build in the willow-trees near the dam, but White Crows, the kind that come only once in many years. As soon as a white crow baby was found, it was taken to Uncle Lion – that was his order; then he kept it in the cliffs of the mountains and let it grow big; and when the old White Crows died the next eldest became watchmen, and so there were always White Crows to watch the bones when Uncle Lion went hunting.

'But one day while he was away Brother Big Bullfrog came along, hop-hop-hoppity-hop, hop-hop-hoppity-hop, and said: "Why do you sit here all day, you Whitehead Crows?"

'And the White Crows said: "We sit here to look after the bones for Uncle Lion."

'"Ach, but you must be tired of sitting!" said Brother Big Bullfrog, "You fly away a little and stretch your wings. I will sit here and look after the bones."

'The White Crows looked this way and that way, up and down and all round, but no! they couldn't see Uncle Lion, and they thought: "Now is our chance to get away for a fly."

'So they said "Cr-r-raw, cr-r-raw!" and stretched out their wings and flew away.

'Brother Big Bullfrog called out after them: "Don't hurry back. Stay as long as you like. I will take care of the bones."

'But as soon as they were gone he said: "Now I shall find out why Uncle Lion keeps the bones from being broken. Now I shall see why men and animals can live no longer."

And he went from one end to the other of Uncle Lion's house at the bottom of the cliff, breaking all the bones he could find.

'Ach, but he worked quickly! Crack! crack, crack, crack! Wherever he went he broke bones. Then when he had finished, he hopped away, hop-hop-hoppity-hop, hop-hop-hoppity-hop, as fast as he could. When he had nearly reached his dam in the veld, the White Crows overtook him. They had been to the cliff and, foy! they were frightened when they saw all the broken bones.

'"Craw, craw!" they said, "Brother Big Bullfrog, why are you so wicked? Uncle Lion will be so angry. He will bite off our nice white heads – craw, craw! – and without a head, who can live?"

'But Brother Big Bullfrog pretended he didn't hear. He just hopped on as fast as he could, and the White Crows went after him.

'"It's no good hopping away, Brother Bullfrog," they said. "Uncle Lion will find you wherever you are, and with one blow of his iron claws he will kill you."

'But old Brother Big Bullfrog didn't take any notice. He just hopped on, and when he came to his dam he sat back at the edge of the water and blinked the beautiful eyes in his ugly old head, and said: "When Uncle Lion comes tell him I am the man who broke the bones. Tell him I live in this dam, and if he wants to see me, he must come here."

'The White Crows were very cross. They flew down quickly to peck Brother Big Bullfrog, but they only dug their beaks into the soft mud, because Brother Big Bullfrog wasn't sitting there any longer. Kabloops! He had dived into the dam, and the White Crows could only see the rings round the place where he had made a hole in the water.

'Uncle Lion was far away in the veld, waiting for food, waiting for food. At last, he saw a herd of zebras – the little striped horses that he is very fond of – and he tried to fly up so that he could fall on one of them, but he couldn't. He tried again, but no, he couldn't. He spread out his wings and flapped them, but they were quite weak, like master's umbrella when the ribs are broken.

'Then Uncle Lion knew there must be something wrong at his house, and he was toch too angry. He struck his iron claws into the ground and roared and roared. Softly he began, like thunder far away rolling through the hills, then louder and louder, till – hoor-rr-rr-rr, hoor-rr-rr-rr – the earth beneath him seemed to shake. It was a terrible noise.

'But all his roaring did not help him, he couldn't fly, and at last he had to get up and walk home. He found the poor White Crows nearly dead with fright, but they soon found out that he could no longer fly, so they were not afraid of him.

'"Hoor-rr-rr-rr, hoor-rr-rr-rr!" he roared. "What have you done to make my wings so weak?"

41

'And they said: "While Uncle was away someone came and broke all the bones."

'And Uncle Lion said: "You were put here to watch them. It is your fault that they are broken, and to punish you I am going to bite your stupid white heads off. Hoor-rr-rr-rr!"

'He sprang towards them, but now that they knew he couldn't fly they were not afraid of him. They flew away and sailed round in the air over his head, just too high for him to reach, and they called out: "Ha! ha! ha! Uncle cannot catch us! The bones are broken, and his wings are useless. Now men and animals can live again. We will fly away and tell them the good news."

'Uncle Lion sprang into the air, first to one side and then to the other, striking at them, but he couldn't reach them, and when he found all his efforts were in vain, he rolled on the ground and roared louder than ever.

'The White Crows flew round him in rings, and called out: "Ha! ha! ha! he can no longer fly! He only rolls and roars!"

'The man who broke the bones said: "If Uncle Lion wants me, he can come and look for me at the dam. Craw, craw," and away they flew.

'Then Uncle Lion thought: "Wait, I'll get hold of the one who broke the bones. I'll get him." So he went to the dam, and there was old Brother Bullfrog sitting in the sun at the water's edge. Uncle Lion crept up slowly, quietly, like a thief, behind Brother Bullfrog.

'"Ha! Now I've got him," he thought, and made a spring, but Brother Bullfrog said,

'"Ho!" and dived in – kabloops! – and came up at the other side of the dam and sat there blinking in the sun.

'Uncle Lion ran round as hard as he could, and was just going to spring, when – kabloops! – Brother Bullfrog dived in again and came up at the other side of the dam.

'And so, it went on. Each time, just when Uncle Lion had nearly caught him, Brother Bullfrog dived in – kabloops! – and called out, "Ho!" from the other side of the dam.

'Then at last Uncle Lion saw it was no use trying to catch Brother Bullfrog, so he went home to see if he could mend the broken bones. But he could not, and from that day he could no longer fly, only walk upon his iron claws. Also, from that day he learned to creep quietly like a thief after his game, and though he still catches them and eats them, he is not as dangerous as he was when he could fly.

'And the White Crows can no longer speak. They can only say, "Craw, craw."

'But old Brother Big Bullfrog still goes hop-hop-hoppity-hop round about the dam, and whenever he sees Uncle Lion he just says, "Ho!" and dives into the water – kabloops! – as fast as he can and sits there laughing when he hears Uncle Lion roar with anger.'

From: Outa Karel's Stories

Godmother Death

THERE WAS A man, very poor in this world's goods, whose wife presented him with a baby boy. No one was willing to stand sponsor, because he was so very poor. The father said to himself:

'Dear Lord, I am so poor that no one is willing to be at my service in this matter; I'll take the baby, I'll go, and I'll ask the first person I meet to act as sponsor, and if I don't meet anybody, perhaps the sexton will help me.'

He went and met Death but didn't know what manner of person she was; she was a handsome woman, like any other woman. He asked her to be godmother. She didn't make any excuse, and immediately saluted him as parent of her godchild, took the baby in her arms, and carried him to church.

The little lad was properly christened. When they came out of church, the child's father took the godmother to an inn, and wanted to give her a little treat as godmother. But she said to him,

'Gossip, leave this alone, and come with me to my abode.' She took him with her to her apartment, which was very handsomely furnished. Afterwards, she conducted him into great vaults, and through these vaults they went right into the under-world in the dark.

There tapers were burning of three sizes – small, large, and middle-sized; and those which were not yet alight were very large.

The godmother said to the godchild's father: 'Look, Gossip, here I have the duration of everybody's life.'

The child's father gazed thereat, found there a tiny taper close to the very ground, and asked her: 'But, Gossip, I pray you, whose is this little taper close to the ground?'

She said to him: 'That is yours! When any taper whatsoever burns down, I must go for that man.'

He said to her: 'Gossip, I pray you, give me somewhat additional.'

She said to him: 'Gossip, I cannot do that!'

Afterwards she went and lighted a large new taper for the baby boy whom they had had christened. Meanwhile, while the godmother was not looking, the child's father took for himself a large new taper, lit it, and placed it where his tiny taper was burning down.

The godmother looked round at him and said:

'Gossip, you ought not to have done that to me; but if you have given yourself additional lifetime, you have done so and possess it. Let us go hence, and we'll go to your wife.'

She took a present and went with the child's father and the child to the mother. She arrived, and placed the boy on his mother's bed, and asked her how she was, and whether she had any pain anywhere. The mother confided her griefs to her, and the father sent for some beer, and wanted to entertain her in his cottage, as godmother, in order to gratify her and show his gratitude. They drank and feasted together. Afterwards the godmother said to her godchild's father:

'Gossip, you are so poor that no one but myself would be at your service in this matter; but never mind, you shall bear me in memory! I will go to the houses of various respectable people and make them ill, and you shall physic and cure them. I will tell you all the remedies. I possess them all, and everybody will be glad to recompense you well, only observe this: When I stand at anyone's feet, you can be of assistance to every such person; but if I stand at anybody's head, don't attempt to aid him.'

It came to pass. The child's father went from patient to patient, where the godmother caused illness, and benefited everyone. All at once he became a distinguished physician. A prince was dying – nay, he had breathed his last – nevertheless, they sent for the physician. He came, he began to anoint him with salves and give him his powders, and did him good. When he had restored him to health, they paid him well, without asking how much they were indebted. Again, a count was dying. They sent for the physician again. The physician came. Death was standing behind the bed at his head.

The physician cried: 'It's a bad case, but we'll have a try.'

He summoned the servants and ordered them to turn the bed round with the patient's feet towards Death, and began to anoint him with salves and administer powders into his mouth, and did him good. The count paid him in return as much as he could carry away, without ever asking how much he was indebted; he was only too glad that he had restored him to health.

When Death met the physician, she said to him: 'Gossip, if this occurs to you again, don't play me that trick any more. True, you have done him good, but only for a while; I must, none the less, take him off whither he is due.'

The child's father went on in this way for some years; he was now very old. But at last, he was wearied out, and asked Death herself to take him. Death was unable to take him, because he had given himself a long additional taper; she was obliged to wait till it burned out. One day he drove to a certain patient to restore him to health and did so. Afterwards Death revealed herself to him and rode with him in his carriage. She began to tickle and play with him and tap him with a green twig under the throat; he threw himself into her lap, and went off into the last sleep. Death laid him in the carriage and took herself off. They found the physician lying dead in his carriage and conveyed him home. The whole town and all the villages lamented: 'That physician is much to be regretted. What a good doctor he was! He was of great assistance; there will never be his like again!' His son remained after him but had not the same skill.

The son went one day into church, and his godmother met him. She asked him: 'My dear son, how are you?'

He said to her: 'Not all alike; so long as I have what my dad saved up for me, it is well with me, but after that the Lord God knows how it will be with me.'

His godmother said: 'Well, my son, fear nought. I am your christening mamma; I helped your father to what he had, and will give you, too, a livelihood. You shall go to a physician as a pupil, and you shall be more skilful than he, only behave nicely.'

After this she anointed him with salve over the ears and conducted him to a physician.

The physician didn't know what manner of lady it was, and what sort of son she brought him for instruction. The lady enjoined her son to behave nicely, and requested the physician to instruct him well, and bring him into a good position. Then she took leave of him and departed. The physician and the lad went together to gather herbs, and each herb cried out to the pupil what remedial virtue it had, and the pupil gathered it. The physician also gathered herbs, but knew not, with regard to any herb, what remedial virtue it possessed. The pupil's herbs were beneficial in every disease.

The physician said to the pupil: 'You are cleverer than I, for I diagnose no one that comes to me; but you know herbs counter to every disease. Do you know what? Let us join partnership. I will give my doctor's diploma up to you, and will be your assistant, and am willing to be with you till death.'

The lad was successful in doctoring and curing till his taper burned out in limbo.

From: Sixty Folk-Tales from Exclusively Slavonic Sources

The Weeoonibeens & the Piggiebillah

Two Weeoombeen brothers went out hunting. One brother was much younger than the other and smaller, so when they sighted an emu, the elder one said to the younger:

'You stay quietly here and do not make a noise, or Piggiebillah, whose camp we passed just now, will hear you and steal the emu if I kill it. He is so strong. I'll go on and try to kill the emu with this stone.'

The little Weeoombeen watched his big brother sneak up to the emu, crawling along, almost flat, on the ground. He saw him get quite close to the emu, then spring up quickly and throw the stone with such an accurate aim as to kill the bird on the spot. The little brother was so rejoiced that he forgot his brother's caution, and he called aloud in his joy. The big Weeoombeen looked round and gave him a warning sign, but too late, Piggiebillah had heard the cry and was hastening towards them. Quickly big Weeoombeen left the emu and joined his little brother.

Piggiebillah, when he came up, said: 'What have you found?'

'Nothing,' said the big Weeoombeen, 'nothing but some mistletoe berries.'

'It must have been something more than that, or your little brother would not have called out so loudly.'

Little Weeoombeen was so afraid that Piggiebillah would find their emu and take it, that he said: 'I hit a little bird with a stone, and I was glad I could throw so straight.'

'It was no cry for the killing of a little bird or for the finding of mistletoe berries that I heard. It was for something much more than either, or you would not have called out so joyfully. If you do not tell me at once I will kill you both.'

The Weeoombeen brothers were frightened, for Piggiebillah was a great fighter and very strong, so when they saw he was really angry, they showed him the dead emu.

'Just what I want for my supper,' he said, and so saying, dragged it away to his own camp. The Weeoombeens followed him and even helped him to make a fire to cook the emu, hoping by so doing to get a share given to them. But Piggiebillah would not give them any; he said he must have it all for himself.

Angry and disappointed, the Weeoombeens marched straight off and told some big fellows who lived near, that Piggiebillah had a fine fat emu just cooked for supper.

Up jumped the big fellows, seized their spears, bade the Weeoombeens quickly lead them to Piggiebillah's camp, promising them for so doing a share of the emu.

When they were within range of spear shot, the big fellows formed a circle, took aim, and threw their spears at Piggiebillah. As the spears fell thick on him, sticking out all over him, Piggiebillah cried aloud: 'Bingehlah, Bingeblah. You can have it; you can have it.'

But the big fellows did not desist until Piggiebillah was too wounded even to cry out; then they left him a mass of spears and turned to look for the emu. But to their surprise they found it not. Then for the first time they missed the Weeoombeens.

Looking around, they saw their tracks going to where the emu had evidently been; then they saw that they had dragged the emu to their nyunnoo, which was a humpy made of grass.

When the Weeoombeens saw the big fellows coming, they caught hold of the emu and dragged it to a big hole they knew of, with a big stone at its entrance, which stone only they knew the secret of moving. They moved the stone, got the emu and themselves into the hole, and the stone in place again before the big fellows reached the place.

The big fellows tried to move the stone but could not. Yet they knew that the Weeoombeens must have done so, for they had tracked them right up to it, and they could hear the sound of their voices on the other side of it. They saw there was a crevice on either side of the stone, between it and the ground. Through these crevices they, drove in their spears, thinking they must surely kill the brothers. But the Weeoombeens too had seen these crevices and had anticipated the spears, so they had placed the dead emu before them to act as a shield. And into its body were driven the spears of the big fellows extended for the Weeoombeens.

Having driven the spears well in, the big fellows went off to get help to move the stone, but when they had gone a little way, they heard the Weeoombeens laughing. Back they came and speared again, and again started for help, only as they left to hear once more the laughter of the brothers.

The Weeoombeens finding their laughter only brought back the big fellows to a fresh attack, determined to keep quiet, which, after the next spearing, they did.

Quite sure, when they heard their spear shots followed by neither conversation nor laughter, that they had killed the Weeoombeens at last, the big fellows hurried away to bring back the strength and cunning of the camp, to remove the stone.

The Weeoombeens hurriedly discussed what plan they had better adopt to elude the big fellows, for well they knew that should they ever meet any of them again they would be killed without mercy. And as they talked, they satisfied their hunger by eating some of the emu flesh.

After a while the big fellows returned, and soon was the stone removed from the entrance. Some of them crept into the hole, where, to their surprise, they found only the remains of the emu and no trace of the Weeoombeens. As those who had gone in first crept out and told of the disappearance of the Weeoombeens, others, incredulous of such a story, crept in to find it confirmed. They searched round for tracks; seeing that their spears were all in the emu it seemed to them probable the Weeoombeens had escaped alive, but if so, whither they had gone their tracks would show. But search as they would no tracks could they find.

All they could see were two little birds which sat on a bush near the hole, watching the big fellows all the time. The little birds flew round the hole sometimes, but never away, always returning to their bush and seeming to be discussing the whole affair; but what they said the big fellows could not understand. But as time went on and no sign was ever found of the Weeoombeens, the big fellows became sure that the brothers had turned into the little white-throated birds which had sat on the bush by the hole, so, they supposed, to escape their vengeance. And ever afterwards the little white-throats were called Weeoombeens. And the memory of Piggiebillah is perpetuated by a sort of porcupine anteater, which bears his name, and whose skin is covered closely with miniature spears sticking all over it.

From: Australian Legendary Tales

The Runaways

THERE WAS ONCE a young man who had journeyed a long way from home in search of adventure. One day he came to a strange village on the border of a great wood, but while yet some distance from the lodges, he happened to glance upward. In the boughs of a tree just above his head, he saw a light scaffold, and on the scaffold a maiden sitting at her needlework.

Instead of boldly entering the village, as he had intended, the youth walked on a little way, then turned and again passed under the tree. He did this several times, and each time he looked up, for the girl was the prettiest that he had ever seen.

He did not show himself to the people, but for several days he lingered on the borders of the wood, and at last he ventured to speak with the maiden and to ask her to be his wife.

She did not seem to be at all unwilling; however, she said to him: 'You must be very careful, for my grandmother does not wish me to marry. She is a very wicked old woman and has thus far succeeded in killing every one of my suitors.'

'In that case, we must run away,' the young man replied. 'Tonight, when your grandmother is asleep, pull up some of the tent-pins and come out. I shall be waiting for you!'

The girl did as he had said, and that same night they fled together and by morning were far from the village.

However, the maiden kept looking over her shoulder as if fearing pursuit, and at last her lover said to her: 'Why do you continue to look behind you? They will not have missed you until daylight, and it is quite certain now that no one can overtake us!'

'Ah,' she replied, 'my grandmother has powerful magic! She can cover a whole day's journey at one step, and I am convinced that she is upon our trail.'

'In that case, you shall see that I, too, know something of magic,' returned the young man. Forthwith he threw down one of his mittens, and lo! Their trail was changed to the trail of a Buffalo. He threw down the other mitten, and it became the carcass of a Buffalo lying at the end of the trail.

'She will follow thus far and no farther,' he declared; but the maiden shook her head and ceased not from time to time to glance over her shoulder as they hastened onward.

In truth it was not long till she perceived the old woman in the distance, coming on with great strides and shaking her cane and her grey head at the runaways.

'Now it is my turn!' the girl exclaimed, and threw down her comb, which became a thick forest behind the fleeing ones, so that the angry old woman was held back by the dense underbrush.

When she had come out of the forest at last and was again gaining upon them, the girl threw her awl over her shoulder and it became a chain of mountains with high peaks and sharp precipices, so that the grandmother was kept back longer than before. Nevertheless, her magic was strong, and she still struggled on after the lovers.

In the meantime, they had come to the bank of a river both wide and deep, and here they stood for a while doubting how they should cross, for there was neither boat nor ford. However, there were two Cranes nearby, and to these the young man addressed himself.

'My friends,' said he, 'I beg of you to stand on the opposite banks of this river and stretch your necks across, so that we may cross in safety! Only do this, and I will give to each of you a fine ornament for your breast, and long fringes on your leggings, so that you will hereafter be called the handsomest of birds!'

The Cranes were willing to oblige, and they stood thus with their beaks touching over the stream, so that the lovers crossed on their long necks in safety.

'Now,' exclaimed the young man, 'I must ask of you one more favour! If an old woman should come down to the river and seek your help, place your heads together once more as if to allow her to cross, but when she is halfway over you must draw back and let her fall in mid-stream. Do this, and I promise you that you shall never be in want!'

In a little while the old woman came down to the river, quite out of breath, and angrier than before. As soon as she noticed the two Cranes, she began to scold and order them about.

'Come here, you long-necks, you ungainly creatures, come and help me over this river!' she cried.

The two Cranes again stood beak to beak, but when the wicked grandmother had crossed halfway, they pulled in their necks and into the water she went, screaming out threats and abuse as she whirled through the air. The current swept her quickly away and she was drowned, for there is no magic so strong that it will prevail against true love.

From: Wigwam Evenings: Sioux Folk Tales Retold

Käthchen & the Kobold

HALFWAY UP THE long steep hill that leads from Soden to Königstein, a rough road branches off to the left, plunging suddenly into a valley, and passing through the little village of Altenhain. As you walk down this steep rocky incline, the Taunus Mountains rise up grand and high in ever-changing panorama.

At the bottom of the hill lies Altenhain, an ordinary enough Taunus village, save for the beautiful shrine that stands on the high road. There a Crucifix hangs between two enormous poplar trees, one of the most beautiful natural altars in the world. The trees are tall and pointed like church spires, the trunks venerable with age. May the lightning spare these grand old trees, and the winds play gently through their boughs!

In this village lived a schoolmaster with his wife and family consisting of a daughter, twelve years old, and a baby boy. They were not really poor, for, besides their income, they had a piece of land to grow potatoes and vegetables; also, a strip of vineyard and fine strawberry fields on the Dachberg, the produce of which they sold in Frankfurt for a good price. Moreover, they kept pigs and chickens and geese, and two dear little goats that gave them milk.

On a fine September day Käthchen (that was the daughter's name) was on the Dachberg, helping her parents to gather up the potatoes for the winter. Two sacks stood already full, looking from a distance like funny old peasants. Käthe liked to watch the potato fires that are lit to burn the refuse of the plants, smouldering and crackling in the dry autumn air, and the smoke curling up in the clear sky.

It was now about five o'clock, and as she had worked all day, she was tired and began to groan and grumble. So her mother said: 'Hurry up and go home now, child, before it gets dark. Fetch the baby (the neighbours had taken charge of it for the day), light the fire, put on the kettle, and peel and boil the potatoes for supper.'

Käthe was only too glad to be let off; her tiredness soon vanished as she flew down the steep, grassy slope of the Dachberg, slipping and tumbling every minute. The sun was low, and glowed through the pines and larches, which stand here together, making a wonderful contrast.

Käthe found her way across the wet emerald field coloured with patches of exquisite lilac from the autumn crocuses growing there in thousands, hanging out their cheeky little orange tongues. She sang and shouted for joy, and a feeling half sadness, half exhilaration, that comes to us often at the twilight, came over her. She wore a little red skirt and loose cotton blouse, and a tidy pinafore put on in order to cover her soiled frock on the way home. Her hair was ash blonde and braided in two plaits round her head. Her eyes were dark and deep-set and were a strange contrast to her hair. She passed over the tiny bridge where the brook crosses the field, and gathered a bunch of wildflowers, meadowsweet and harebells, water forget-me-nots and ragged robin, and made a pretty nosegay. She also picked a graceful spray of hops, the leaves slightly tinged with red, and wound it in and out of her hair. She had forgotten the baby and the supper and all the things for which she was responsible and was just a little maiden living in her own enchanted land.

Now the path wound close by the pine woods, and the air seemed to grow chillier and more solemn. She saw great white clouds resting on the Dachberg above her. She seemed so far away, down in this valley and so alone. But she knew that her father and mother were near, probably watching her from the hilltop; it was silly to be frightened, she knew the way so well.

Suddenly something sprang out of the bushes on to the path in front of her. She gave a great jump, but then so did he and she saw that it was only an old green frog. He cheered her up at once, and she began to poke at him with a stick and to sing:

> 'The frog sits in the rushes,
> The funny fat old man,
> And sings his evening ditties
> As sweetly as he can,
> Quark – Quark – Quark.'

But as suddenly as he had appeared on the scene, the frog vanished again with a leap and a bound into the dark waters of the little brook that ran along by the side of the way.

Then she heard a rustling of the bushes and saw a little red squirrel peering at her with his bright, inquisitive eyes.

Round and round the tree-trunk he went, enjoying himself thoroughly, and making fun of Käthchen, playing peep-bo like a baby.

The sun glowed through the tree trunks. It must be about six o'clock.

'I must hurry up or supper will not be ready when my father and mother come home,' she thought.

She then became aware of the sound of footsteps coming towards her along the path.

'Probably a peasant from Altenhain,' she thought, and was pleased to think of meeting a friend. But the footsteps sounded strange and light, more like the pattering of raindrops through leaves, and then for a moment, she turned giddy; it seemed to her as if the trees were really rushing past her, as they seem to do when we look at them out of a railway carriage. One of the young oak trees seemed to be running towards her down the path; but as she looked more closely, and her head became steadier, she saw that it was a boy a little older than herself, who came running towards her, and very queer he looked.

He had a great mass of brown curly hair tumbling about his head; green ears – it seemed to her, could it be possible? No, it must be that he had stuck oak leaves into his curly locks for ornament, pretty oak leaves tinged with soft red. Moreover, he had the bluest and strangest eyes she had ever seen. They shone like wonderful jewels at one moment, and then turned dull and opaque and looked almost dead. He had on rough green trousers, and a white shirt with yellow embroidered braces; his feet were bare and very brown. When he saw Käthe, he gave a wild kind of Indian whoop, and danced round and round her. Much to the poor child's dismay, his eyes flashing all sorts of colours. Her heart beat fast, but not a word or sound would come out of her mouth.

The boy then made a deep bow and took her by the hand. Soon he had his long arms round her waist and was trying to kiss her.

Käthe began to cry with fear and indignation, 'You rude, naughty boy,' she said, 'I will tell my mother of you.'

The imp seemed much surprised, caught one of her tears on his finger, held it up to the light and then sucked it, making funny faces all the time. Käthe could not help laughing, and then she dried her tears with a corner of her apron. She sat down on a tree-trunk for a moment and tried to think.

Immediately the boy sat by her and begged her to give him a kiss. He looked quite nice and pretty for the moment, and Käthe thought she had better do as he wished, or he might begin his antics again. So, she gave him a motherly kiss, just as she would give to her baby brother, smack on the cheek. Immediately the queer look went out of his eyes, and a more human expression took its place.

'Käthe,' he said, 'Käthe, I am but a lonely little imp of the forest, but I love you, Käthe, and I want you to marry me, and live with me always, and be my own little wife. Will you, O will you? O do, do, do,' he said, dancing up and down in wild excitement.

'O goodness gracious me, you are certainly quite crazy,' said Käthe, 'I will tell my mother of you!' She began to cry again and smacked him whenever he tried to come near her.

Then he seized her by the hand and dragged her after him into the wild woods, till they were lost in the forest.

'O dear, O dear, whatever shall I do? What will mother say when she finds no Käthe, no supper, and no baby. Boo-o-o-o!'

'Never mind,' said our imp consolingly, 'you can't help it now, you have run away with me you see.'

'I didn't, indeed I didn't,' interrupted Käthe indignantly.

'I will send a moonshine Käthchen to take your place for the night. You are fond of dreaming, aren't you?'

'O yes, mother often calls me 'Träum Lies' (Dreaming Liese).'

'Well then, it's all right, she will not notice anything, and you and I will have fine times together. If you won't marry me, at least, we can get engaged you know, that will be fine fun.'

'Hum, 'said Käthe, 'that would be amusing. We might play at being engaged! that would not matter. Have you a gold ring for me?'

'O we will go and buy one at the flower shop,' said he.

'At the flower shop, that is a funny place to buy rings at,' said Käthe.

'Buttercups and dandelions melted to a yellow heat make splendid fairy gold,' he replied.

'Ah, then you really are a fairy!' said the little girl.

'Why of course, did you think I was a human child like you? What did they teach you at school?'

'Reading, writing and arithmetic, history and geography and scripture and sewing,' said Käthe.

'But not how to know a fairy when you see one, O my stars!' said our hero.

> 'What is the good of learning
> To read and write and sew,
> To count and do addition
> If fairies you don't know?
>
> How do you know a fairy?
> O by his glittering eye,
> And by his light, light footsteps
> You know when he goes by.
>
> O what are school and lessons,
> My little maiden, pray,
> If to the land of fairy
> They do not show the way?'

So, he sang, and Käthchen thought to herself: 'I've always suspected that we did not learn everything at school.'

By this time her little head was completely turned; she thought no more of supper or mother or baby, but only wondered with round eyes what would happen next.

The moon shone brilliantly through the branches, and she noticed that the trees began to move, and some of them quickly changed places.

'Have you ever seen the trees dance?' said our hero.

We will call him Green Ears; for I had forgotten to say that being a tree-imp, his ears were shaped like oak leaves, and were green tinged with pinky red. It was peculiar of course, but not so very noticeable on account of his thick curly hair. He was able to move them if anything startled him, to prick up his ears in very truth; then you saw that they really belonged to him.

The trees did not wait for Käthe to reply; they formed themselves in long avenues and began a stately dance, something like a quadrille.

A soft fairy music was played by an invisible band. Squirrels sprang at intervals from one tree to another, spreading out their bushy tails and uttering strange cries like newborn babies.

Birds flew in and out singing and keeping time to the music and rhythm of the dance. It was a strange sight, grotesque yet beautiful; the trees took half human forms and faces; it was funny to see how they joined hands (or branches) from time to time in the dance. After they had watched for some time and the sport had become monotonous, Green Ears took Käthe to the top of the hill, and there they saw the beautiful, peaked mountain called the Rossert, bathed in the moonlight.

'Well, children, enjoying yourselves on this fine night, I hope?' said a woman of tall and commanding presence.

'Will you come home and have supper with me? I am sure Green Ears has forgotten to offer you anything to eat.'

Here she chucked him under his pointed chin.

The two children, fairy and human, turned and followed her, they felt that she was a person of authority and must be obeyed. Her fair hair fell in waving masses almost to her feet, it was covered with soft feathers, as if she had recently been filling feather beds.

The children saw a lighted cottage before them, with red roof and black-beamed walls like so many in the Taunus. A strong smell of honeysuckle was wafted towards them.

'This is my wood cottage, it is quite close to the Rossert, as you see. Some people call me the wood-woman, others Frau Holle,' she said.

'The Old King (the mountain called Altkönig) is my brother; Olle (slang in German for old) or Holle, it is all the same, we are all relations in the Taunus, you must know!'

In front of the house was a dear little garden. The moonlight shone brightly on the flowerbeds. The fairies were awake and peeped out with the greatest interest as the children entered.

Over the door was written in letters made of light, like those beautiful advertisements of beer and chocolate which so adorn the city of London by night:

THIS WAY TO FAIRYLAND

Käthe felt that she was learning more in one night than in all her life before of that strange dreamworld on the borders of which we live.

The house was so neat and tidy, that it looked as if it had just been spring-cleaned; the windows stood wide open, the moonlight streamed in. A little table was laid for supper.

Frau Holle invited them to sit down, and they did so at once.

Green Ears sat opposite to Käthe, staring at her with a wistful expression of adoration and love in his eyes.

A chocolate pudding with cream and sugar and a bilberry jelly stood on the table, also rolls which were thickly buttered and spread with various kinds of fairy sausage, purely vegetarian in character. Mugs of delicious-looking milk were ready for each child.

But the supper reminded Käthe of her home and she felt a little uneasy.

However, she had at the bottom of all a comfortable feeling that all was right. This is the way with many of our self-imposed troubles, big people's as well as little people's. We groan and grumble, and express our views that everything is very wrong, and the world is soon going to the dogs, but at the bottom of all, we know that it is all right, and that all things work together for good.

Green Ears began to fidget—he was like a little girl I know—and could not sit still for more than one minute.

'Frau Holle,' he said, 'Frau Holle, Gracious Lady, we want to get engaged.'

Frau Holle burst out laughing: 'A mortal child and a Kobold of the forest! nonsense, it's impossible!'

Käthchen lifted up her brown eyes. 'We might play at it,' she said. 'It would be a beautiful game.'

Frau Holle chuckled so much at this that she nearly upset the milk jug.

'How do people get engaged?' said Käthe. 'I have often thought about it, but I never could imagine how they do it?'

'Didn't they teach you that at school either?' said Green Ears. 'My stars! What did they teach you at school?'

'Children,' said the wood-woman, 'children, do you mean it?'

'Certainly,' said Green Ears.

'I think so,' said Käthe.

'Do you wish to buy rings?'

'O yes,' decidedly from both children.

'Now listen; there is a passage from my house leading to the shops, most convenient, I assure you,' said Frau Holle. 'Everything delivered punctually on the premises within one minute of purchasing it. No lifts or motorcars necessary. You see, I know the ways of the world.'

So saying, she opened the back door, and they passed into a lane lighted by many lampposts. These gave a very bright light and had queer faces like the man in the moon. They grinned and winked as Green Ears and Käthchen went by.

It was a lovely fair; a fair in fairyland you may imagine how gorgeous that must be!

There were stalls on which lay all sorts of tempting things, cakes, sweet and toys. Käthe felt sorry that she had no money.

At the flower stall they paused; the flowers were exquisitely arranged, and out of each peeped a little Fee.

In big gold letters was written:

CONDENSED FLOWERS FOR SALE.

As Green Ears asked boldly for engagement rings, a fairy who stood behind the stall handed him two little gold rings made to fit any finger; they were a new patent and self-adapting, the fairy said.

Green Ears was so pleased that he turned head over heels again and again for joy, a funny proceeding for a would-be husband.

'Do you know how to get engaged,' he said to the fairy.

'Why no, not exactly, but I have heard it is very simple,' said she. 'Mother Holle (here she made a deep curtsy), Mother Holle knows all about it.'

Käthe looked out of the corner of her eyes at her lover, and wished he would behave with more dignity. Now he was cramming his mouth with sweeties.

'Aren't you going to give me any?' she said.

'O my stars!' he said again, surprised; it had never struck him. Imps are usually egoists; they think first of themselves. There are exceptions, but this is the rule.

He went rapidly from stall and returned with his arms full of parcels done up in pink paper, which he presented to Käthchen with a low bow. She accepted them with much delight, and they fell to munching chocolate together; it was a real bond of union, and they were not the first sweethearts who discovered it.

They reached the end of the street and suddenly found themselves alone once more on the slopes of the Altenhainer Thal or Valley.

Green Ears sat down by Käthchen, and squeezed himself up closely to her.

'Give me your pretty little hand,' he said. 'Do you know which is the right finger?'

'O yes!' Käthchen knew that quite well, though I have heard that it is a disputed point in Germany.

She stuck out her little hard-worked fingers, and he put the gold ring on the third finger of the left hand. It fitted exactly and with a cry of joy Käthchen put the other on his long brown finger.

Then both the children laughed and clapped their hands and danced merrily about.

'Now we are engaged,' they cried, 'really engaged to be married!'

They made such a noise that the squirrels were cross and threw sticks at them for disturbing their early-morning sleep.

Then, goodness knows why – let us call it reaction – Käthe began to cry again, great, big drops.

Green Ears was much puzzled. 'You are clever, now I can't do that,' he said. 'You must stay with me always, and live with me in the woods, and be my own little sweetheart.'

'O no,' said Käthe, 'I should never be allowed to do that; I must go to school every day, and then I have my exercises to do, and to help mother with the housework; the baby to mind; and – O I am always so busy.'

'I will come and help you,' said Green Ears.

'But you can't, you are not real, you know,' said Käthe and began to cry again.

'Käthchen,' said Green Ears, and he looked quite serious and thinky all at once. 'Listen to me. I will go to the Old King; he is the ruler of all the fairies here, and I will beg him to teach me how to become human. It may be years before we meet again, for the way into your world is very hard for me to find. Yes, it is easier for you to find the way into our world, than for us to enter yours; but cheer up, I will dare it and do it for your sake! but O sweetheart wait for me; O wait for me!'

'Wait for me, my little sweetheart,
Till I come to you again,
Win the world for you, my sweetheart,
With its joy and with its pain.

Wait for me, my little sweetheart,
For when falling on the ground
I beheld those curious dewdrops
To your heart my heart was bound.

All my fairy life is nothing,
All my fairy joy I give,
Just to hold your hands, my sweetheart,
In your world with you to live.

Wait for me, my little sweetheart:
I will find the way to you,
As a grown man I will seek you,
Seek and find you ever true.'

So singing, they walked arm in arm through the long winding valley, till the dawn approached like a golden bird opening its great wings to fly.

Käthchen reached her cottage door. All was silent within.

'Good-bye,' she said, and their eyes met in one last farewell.

'Auf Wiedersehen!' said Green Ears (that pretty German farewell which means so much more than goodbye), and then he stole back down the stony street, kissing his hands again and again to the little girl.

In some strange way, Käthchen passed through the door of her little cottage; she had become for the time incorporeal; through the touch of a fairy her body and soul had become loose, that is to say, and she was able to enter the house as silently as a person in a dream. She went through the kitchen and up the steep wooden stairs. It seemed to her as if her feet did not touch the ground, she floated rather than walked. She reached her own little attic and saw the room as if it were a picture, the square windowframe, the branches of the trees outside, the old pictures on the walls that she was so fond of.

But what was her surprise to see herself curled up asleep in her big wooden bed!

The horror of it made her faint, and she remembered no more until she found herself in her own bed under her own big feather sack. In order that she should not forget her night's adventures, or think it was all merely a dream, she found a ring of yellow grass wound tightly round her third finger. From that hour, though the ring fell to pieces, the mark of it was clearly to be seen on her finger. It was a fairy ring, you see.

Her mother apparently had not missed her, and the baby was as jolly as ever.

'What was the matter with you last night, Käthe?' said her mother. 'You were dreamier than ever; not a word could we get out of you. You must have been tired out, you poor child!'

'But everything was all right, wasn't it, mother, the potatoes were boiled and the supper ready?'

'Why, of course, you managed very nicely. Now hurry up and let us have breakfast.'

Now I feel sure that all the children who read this story will want to know what happened to Käthchen and Green Ears later on.

Did he really come back to visit her as a grown man?

Did they marry and live happy ever after?

Had he green ears as a mortal?

But alas, the fairies who told me this story have left these questions unanswered—at all events for the present—so I can only guess at the conclusion.

I think myself that Green Ears was pretty sure to succeed in his quest, because if you want a thing intensely enough, you can usually get it.

They would make a rather funny married couple, that is true, and we will hope that Green Ears did not turn head over heels on his marriage day.

But the fairies assure me that the trials necessary to pass through in order to become a mortal have a very sobering effect on the character, and so we can think of Green Ears as quite different, though still fascinating and charming.

I would have liked to be present at their wedding, wouldn't you?

'O joy when on this solid earth
Is heard the sound of fairy mirth!
O joy, when under earthly things
Is heard the sound of fairy wings,
When the impossible is true,
When I come back and marry you!'

From: Fairy Tales from the German Forests

The Husband Who Was to
Mind the House

ONCE ON A time there was a man, so surly and cross, he never thought his Wife did anything right in the house. So, one evening, in haymaking time, he came home, scolding and swearing, and showing his teeth and making a dust.

'Dear love, don't be so angry; there's a good man,' said his goody; 'tomorrow let's change our work. I'll go out with the mowers and mow, and you shall mind the house at home.'

Yes! The Husband thought that would do very well. He was quite willing, he said.

So, early next morning, his goody took a scythe over her neck, and went out into the hayfield with the mowers, and began to mow; but the man was to mind the house and do the work at home.

First of all, he wanted to churn the butter; but when he had churned a while, he got thirsty, and went down to the cellar to tap a barrel of ale. So, just when he had knocked in the bung, and was putting the tap into the cask, he heard overhead the pig come into the kitchen.

Then off he ran up the cellar steps, with the tap in his hand, as fast as he could, to look after the pig, lest it should upset the churn; but when he got up, and saw the pig had already knocked the churn over, and stood there, routing and grunting amongst the cream which was running all over the floor, he got so wild with rage that he quite forgot the ale barrel, and ran at the pig as hard as he could. He caught it, too, just as it ran out of doors, and gave it such a kick, that piggy lay for dead on the spot. Then all at once he remembered he had the tap in his hand; but when he got down to the cellar, every drop of ale had run out of the cask.

Then he went into the dairy and found enough cream left to fill the churn again, and so he began to churn, for butter they must have at dinner. When he had churned a bit, he remembered that their milking cow was still shut up in the byre and hadn't had a bit to eat or a drop to drink all the morning, though the sun was high.

Then all at once he thought 'twas too far to take her down to the meadow, so he'd just get her up on the house top – for the house, you must know, was thatched with sods, and a fine crop of grass was growing there. Now the house lay close up against a steep down, and he thought if he laid a plank across to the thatch at the back, he'd easily get the cow up.

But still he couldn't leave the churn, for there was his little babe crawling about on the floor, and 'if I leave it,' he thought, 'the child is safe to upset it.' So he took the churn on his back, and went out with it; but then he thought he'd better first water the cow before he turned her out on the thatch; so he took up a bucket to draw water out of the well; but, as he stooped down at the well's brink, all the cream ran out of the churn over his shoulders, and so down into the well.

Now it was near dinnertime, and he hadn't even got the butter yet; so he thought he'd best boil the porridge, and filled the pot with water and hung it over the fire.

When he had done that, he thought the cow might perhaps fall off the thatch and break her legs or her neck. So, he got up on the house to tie her up. One end of the rope he made fast to the cow's neck and the other he slipped down the chimney and tied round his own thigh; and he had to make haste, for the water now began to boil in the pot, and he had still to grind the oatmeal.

So, he began to grind away; but while he was hard at it, down fell the cow off the house-top after all, and as she fell, she dragged the man up the chimney by the rope. There he stuck fast; and as for the cow, she hung halfway down the wall, swinging between heaven and earth, for she could neither get down nor up.

And now the goody had waited seven lengths and seven breadths for her Husband to come and call them home to dinner; but never a call they had. At last, she thought she'd waited long enough, and went home. But when she got there and saw the cow hanging in such an ugly place, she ran up and cut the rope in two with her scythe. But, as she did this, down came her Husband out of the chimney; and so, when his old dame came inside the kitchen, there she found him standing on his head in the porridge pot.

From: East of the Sun and West of the Moon

The Eagles

There was once a king who had lost his wife. They had a family of thirteen: twelve gallant sons, and one daughter, who was exquisitely beautiful.

For twelve years after his wife's death, the king grieved very much; he used to go daily to her tomb, and there weep, and pray, and give away alms to the poor. He thought never to marry again; for he had promised his dying wife never to give her children a stepmother.

One day, when visiting his dead wife's grave as usual, he saw beside him a maiden so entrancingly fair, that he fell in love with her, and soon made her his second queen. But before long he found out that he had made a great mistake. Though she was so beautiful, she turned out to be a wicked sorceress, and not only made the king himself unhappy, but proved most unkind to his children, whom she wished out of the way, so that her own little son might inherit the kingdom.

One day, when the king was far away, at war against his enemies, the queen went into her stepchildren's apartments, and pronounced some magical words – on which every one of the twelve princes flew away in the shape of an eagle, and the princess was changed into a dove.

The queen looked out of the window, to see in what direction they would fly, when she saw right under the window an old man, with a beard as white as snow.

'What are you here for, old man?' she asked.

'To be witness of your deed,' he answered.

'Then you saw it?'

'I saw it.'

'Then be what I command!'

She whispered some magical words. The old man disappeared in a blaze of sunshine; and the queen, as she stood there, dumb with terror, was changed into a basilisk.

The basilisk ran off in fright; trying to hide herself underground. But her glance was so deadly, that it killed everyone she looked at; so that all the people in the palace were soon dead, including her own son, whom she slew by merely looking at him. And this once populous and happy royal residence quickly became an uninhabited ruin, which no one dared approach, for fear of the basilisk lurking in its underground vaults.

Meanwhile the princess, who had been changed into a dove, flew after her brothers the eagles, but not being able to overtake them, she rested under a wayside cross, and began cooing mournfully.

'What are you grieving for, pretty dove?' asked an old man, with a snow-white beard, who just then came by.

'I am grieving for my poor dear father, who is fighting in the wars far away; for my loved brothers, who have flown away from me into the clouds. I am grieving also for myself. Not long ago I was a happy princess; and now I must wander over the world as a dove, to hide from the birds of prey – and be parted forever from my dear father and brothers!'

'You may grieve and weep, little dove; but do not lose hope,' said the old man. 'Sorrow is only for a time, and all will come right in the end.'

So saying, he stroked the little dove, and she at once regained her natural shape. She kissed the old man's hand in her gratitude, saying: 'How can I ever thank you enough! But since you are so kind, will you not tell me how to rescue my brothers?'

The old man gave her an ever-growing loaf, and said: 'This loaf is enough to sustain not only you, but a thousand people for a thousand years, without ever diminishing. Go towards the sunset and weep your tears into this little bottle. And when it is full...'

And the old man told her what else to do, blessed her, and disappeared.

The princess travelled on towards the sunset; and in about a year she reached the boundary of the next world, and stood before an iron door, where Death was keeping guard with his scythe.

'Stop, princess!' he said; 'You can proceed no further, for you are not yet parted by death from your own world.'

'But what am I to do?' she asked. 'Must I go back without my poor brothers?'

'Your brothers,' said Death, 'fly here every day in the guise of eagles. They want to reach the other side of this door, which leads into the other world; for they hate the one they live in; nevertheless, they, and you also, must remain there, until your time become. Therefore, every day I must compel them to go back, which they can do, because they are eagles. But how are you going to get back yourself? – look there!'

The princess looked around her and wept bitterly. For though she had not perceived this before, nor seen how she got there, she saw now that she was in a deep abyss, shut in on all sides by such high precipices, that she wondered how her brothers, even with eagle wings, could fly to the top.

But remembering what the mysterious old man had said, she took courage and began to pray and weep, till she had filled the little bottle with her tears. Soon she heard the sound of wings over her head and saw twelve eagles flying.

The eagles dashed themselves against the iron portal, beating their wings upon it, and imploring Death to open it to them. But Death only threatened them with his scythe, saying: 'Hence! ye enchanted princes! you must fulfil your penance on earth, till I come for you myself.'

The eagles were about to turn and fly when all at once they perceived their sister. They came round her and caressed her hands lovingly with their beaks.

She at once began to sprinkle them with her tears from the lachrymatory; and in one moment the twelve eagles were changed back into the twelve princes, and joyfully embraced their sister.

The princess then fed them all round from her ever-growing loaf; but when their hunger was appeased, they began to be troubled as to how they were to ascend from the abyss, since they had no longer eagles' wings to fly up.

But the princess knelt down and prayed: 'Bird of heavenly pity here, By each labour, prayer and tear, Come in thine unvanquished power, Come and aid us in this hour!'

And all at once there shot down from heaven to the depth of the abyss a ray of sunshine, on which descended a gigantic bird, with rainbow wings, a bright sparkling crest, and peacock's eyes all over his body, a golden tail, and silvery breast.

'What are your commands, princess?' asked the bird.

'Carry us from this threshold of eternity to our own world.'

'I will, but you must know, princess, that before I can reach the top of this precipice with you on my back, three days and nights must pass; and I must have food on the way, or my strength will fail me, and I shall fall down with you to the bottom, and we shall all perish.'

'I have an ever-growing loaf, which will suffice both for you and ourselves,' replied the princess.

'Then climb upon my back, and whenever I look around, give me some bread to eat.'

The bird was so large that all the princes, and the princess in the midst of them, could easily find place on his back, and he began to fly upwards.

He flew higher and higher, and whenever he looked around at her, she gave him bits of the loaf, and he flew on, and upwards.

So, they went on steadily for two nights and days; but upon the third day, when they were hoping in a short time to view the summit of the precipice, and to land upon the borders of this world, the bird looked around as usual for a piece of the loaf.

The princess was just going to break off some to give him, when a sudden violent gust of wind from the bottom of the abyss snatched the loaf from her hand and sent it whistling downwards.

Not having received his usual meal the bird became sensibly weaker and looked around once more.

The princess trembled with fear; she had nothing more to give him, and she felt that he was becoming exhausted. In utter desperation she cut off a piece of her flesh and gave it to him. Having eaten this the bird recovered strength and flew upwards faster than before; but after an hour or two he looked around once more.

So, she cut off another piece of her flesh; the bird seized it greedily and flew on so fast that in a few minutes he reached the ground at the top of the precipice. When they alighted, and he asked her: 'Princess, what were those two delicious morsels you gave me last? I never ate anything so good before.'

'They were part of my flesh, I had nothing else for you,' replied the princess in a faint voice, for she was swooning away with pain and loss of blood. The bird breathed upon her wounds; and the flesh at once healed over and grew again as before. Then he flew up again to heaven and was lost in the clouds.

The princess and her brothers resumed their journey, this time towards the sunrise, and at last arrived in their own country, where they met their father, returning from the wars.

The king was coming back victorious over his enemies, and on his way home had first heard of the sudden disappearance of his children and of the queen, and how his palace was tenanted only by a basilisk with a death-dealing glance.

He was therefore most surprised and overjoyed to meet his dear children once more, and on the way his daughter told him all that had come to pass.

When they got back to the palace the king sent one of his nobles with a looking glass down into the underground vaults. The basilisk saw herself reflected in this mirror, and her own glance slew her immediately.

They gathered up the remains of the basilisk and burnt them in a great fire in the courtyard, afterwards scattering the ashes to the four winds. When this was done, the king, his sons, and his daughter, returned to live in their former home and were all as happy as could be ever after.

From: Polish Fairy Tales

About Bears: By One of Them

I COME OF what those conceited creatures, the humans, would probably call humble parentage. In other words, I belong to the great Ursine family: I am a bear. I may as well say at once, in order that there may be no misunderstandings between the humans and myself, in case my life story should ever come into their hands, that I do not in the slightest degree share their opinion as to the relative position in the scale of existence occupied respectively by them and by me.

Indeed, if they will excuse my saying so, in my humble judgment I am at least as good as they are, and perhaps a little better. For instance, to compare us physically, I am taller than many, and broader, stronger, braver, fleeter, more majestic than the best of them. A human is a mere toy in my hands, as I have proved over and over again – why, there was old Ivan the keeper, only last month, he – but I am digressing. Ha! I can't help laughing, though, when I recall poor Ivan's face as I hugged him – me! How his tongue did stick out!

Again, if we are compared intellectually, I very much doubt whether we bears are so inferior as my friends the humans suppose. We do not talk their language – true! But, do they talk ours? I think not. On the other hand, we understand theirs – while they are ignorant altogether of ours!

As for their sciences, their education, their 'ologies (which they think so much of), their arts, their wars, their politics, their freedom – freedom! Ha ha! It is not our notion of freedom! – do all these things render them the happier? What has all this 'civilisation,' so called, done for them? Are they freer than I am? Do they get more to eat and drink, and pay less for their victuals?

Well, well! I must not continue in this strain, airing my pet ideas instead of proceeding with what I intended to be a mere record of my own personal career; I could say much in support of the opinion expressed at the beginning of this chapter: namely, that we bears are just as good, if not a little better, than the human race; but then, after all, I shall never succeed in convincing the conceited – the most conceited of all creatures – man, of his inferiority: as for my ursine readers; – well, we know what we know!

My earliest recollections are among the most painful of all those scenes of my life which have impressed themselves upon my memory; for they are connected with the murder of my dear mother – the base and barbarous murder of as good and indulgent a mother as ever brought into the world and nourished a promising little Bruin family, for such, I think, my small brothers and sisters and I may fairly be called. I will record the shocking circumstances of our great domestic tragedy exactly as they occurred. My earliest recollections are of life in a dark and confined space in which my two brothers and my two sisters and I had but little room for our juvenile recreations. I remember a dear old mother who divided her time in sleeping and admonishing and educating us. We were born in this place, she told us; it was called a 'berloga,' and was the den she had prepared for herself as a shelter during the long months of a cold and cruel Russian winter.

It was not cold inside this den of ours, on the contrary, it was very warm indeed. We had been born in December, and between that month and March we had had plenty of time to grow – we little ones – so that the berloga, which had been amply large enough for my mother alone, had become what I may describe as a tight fit for the six of us. It was lucky, mother used to say, that father was not with us at the time. He was away – she did not seem to know where, exactly, but she had arranged to meet him near a certain village, whose name she mentioned, sometime in spring.

I remember our mother used often to say, 'Do let me go to sleep now, my dears; when you are older you will understand how difficult it is to keep awake in the winter time after the fatigues of a long season!' and, indeed, the good soul used frequently to fall fast asleep in the very midst of our lesson time – much to our joy, for we were always ready for a game of romps in that heyday time of childhood. Mother would have slept the whole winter but for us brats, she used to tell us! Well, one day about the end of March, when the other children and I were busily engaged in rolling over one another, and pretending to worry each other's ears, which was a favourite game of ours, we heard a terrible noise outside.

Up to this time we had never heard any sound at all excepting such as we made ourselves. There were shouts and barking of dogs, and a creature – whom I afterwards discovered to be a human – was knocking at the sides of our house with a long pole – we could see all this through a small peephole which we kept open. We also saw other human creatures standing nearby. These last held in their hands steel sticks clubbed at one end and were looking straight into the mouth of the den. Mother was fast asleep, and we were obliged to awake her, for we felt alarmed at the aspect of these human creatures, puny beings though they seemed when compared with our beloved parent, who was so very much larger and stronger than they.

Mother started up and rubbed her eyes: 'What is it, you tiresome children?' she asked.

Just at this moment, she caught sight of the man who, with his pole, was pushing and striking at the snowed-up mouth of the berloga. Immediately mother's face and form changed. I had never seen her look as she now did. Her beautiful brown coat stood out and her ears went back. Red blood came into her eyes, and her claws stretched out to their full length. She growled savagely, and for a moment or two glared at the human disturber of her peace as though she would every instant rush out and tear him limb from limb.

At last, she spoke to us: 'Children,' she said, 'we are in great danger, and I know not what best to do: you are so young to take care of yourselves!'

'Take care of ourselves, mother?' we said – 'what do you mean! you are not going to leave us?'

'Not if I can help it, dears,' said my mother, licking and caressing us each in turn, as she spoke: 'but do you see the sticks which yonder men hold in their hands? those are called guns; they are terrible things, and spit fire and smoke at us bears. But for them, I should fall upon these human miscreants, and we should sup upon their flesh – which is very good eating, and some bears prefer it to a vegetable diet. As it is, I shall spring first at this man with the pole – he cannot hurt me. Then I shall attack the others; but, dear children, it is very dangerous, for the contest is unequal; those fire-sticks may kill me before I reach them. If they do, you must all stay as still as mice in here – perhaps they will not see you. Should they see you, you must run for it; keep behind the trees, and don't run across the snow patches, of which there are still some about, for that will leaves traces of the direction you have taken, and you may be followed. If you escape, find some lair for yourselves, and keep together for warmth. Eat what you can find. And now, dear children, we must part: if I escape with my life I shall soon return and find you; if not, good-bye – don't forget your mother and all her advice!'

With these words our dear mother suddenly sprang out of the berloga, and in an instant had knocked down the human who was the nearest to us – him with the pole. Then without waiting a second, she hurled herself upon the other two creatures, those which held the fire-sticks, or guns. Instantly there was a terrific noise, like a clap of thunder, but shorter and louder; followed by a second and a third. But mother had reached the nearer of the two humans and had risen on her hind feet with such a roar that even we, her children, were startled and frightened. She seemed to reach and claw at him – oh! How majestic and grand she looked compared with her puny antagonist. Then she and he fell over together, and I saw the second creature point his fire-stick at them as they rolled on the ground; it spat out its fire again, and mother rose and disappeared among the trees! Dear, brave mother! What a glorious fight she made of it – and she had escaped after all, then! Good, brave mother!

Very soon we saw the pole-man rise and rub his head, and he and the third man creature went together to look at the second, who was lying as mother had left him, upon the ground. They did not seem to be able to mend him, however, for he still lay on and took no notice of them. But all this time a horrid little white creature who was with them, a thing called a dog, had been poking around our den with its tail tucked tightly between its hind legs – an ugly and silly habit of these creatures when they feel alarmed. He was sniffing about the mouth of the lair, and suddenly – entering a foot or two further than he had ventured before – caught sight of one of my sisters. He instantly turned and ran out of the berloga as fast as he could lay his wretched thin legs to the ground, barking and yelping, and my silly little sister, unable to resist the temptation, must needs run after him. Immediately there was another explosion from the man with the fire-stick, and poor little Katia, my sister, rolled over and over and then lay quite still – dead; murdered!

'Here! Ivan!' cried the man, 'go into the berloga and see if there are more of the little brutes – try and catch one or two alive for the Zoo!'

It was all up! Ivan came blundering into our house, groping about with his hands, for it was too dark to see anything. We all lay still, for we were too small to hurt him, and we hoped to escape. But his hand came in contact with little Mishka's coat and Ivan held on tight, in spite of poor Mishka's struggles and snarls and bites. The rest of us, not wishing to lose our freedom, rushed out of the lair, leaving Mishka in Ivan's hands, a captive. As we darted out and made for the shelter of the trees, remembering mother's advice, the dreadful fire-stick spat out its fire and smoke at us, but none of us were hurt by it, and Vainka, Natasha, and I got safely away and huddled ourselves together inside the trunk of an old dead pine tree. Here we stayed for hours, not daring to move for fear of being found by the cruel humans and their fire-sticks. When it began to grow dark, we ventured out and crept back to the berloga. There was no sign of the humans; poor dead Katia had been taken away and little prisoner Mishka also; but where was mother?

We wandered about calling for her in all directions; at last – just as we were giving up the search for the night – Natasha heard a sound which she said she was sure was our dear mother crying. Then we all listened and heard it and proceeding in the direction from which it seemed to come, we found poor dear mother lying stretched upon the ground, bleeding and weak. She had three horrible wounds, all given by those detestable fire-spitting sticks called guns, and her lifeblood was fast oozing from them.

'I am dying, my children,' she said – 'are you all safe?' She looked around at us, with her poor glazing eyes, and noticed that some were missing.

'Where are Katia and Mishka?' she asked.

We were obliged to tell the sad truth.

Again, we saw that dreadful look of savage hatred come over mother's face. For a few moments she could say nothing; then at last she muttered: 'Promise me, children, that throughout your lives you will hate and fight mankind, wherever you meet his detested offspring! promise me this, and I shall die happy!'

We all promised faithfully to do as she wished. These were dear mother's last words to us, and a few moments later she died, and her soul flew away to those happy hunting-grounds where, as we bears are taught to believe, it is our part to handle the fire-sticks, and that of the human beings to be hunted!

Thus, we lost our dear mother, together with a small sister and brother whom we could better spare. Considering the circumstances of our deprivation, by means of the foulest murder, of a parent's care and authority, and of our last promise to a beloved and dying mother, is it to be wondered at that I can never cherish any other feeling towards that archenemy of my family – man, than hatred, and that of the deepest? My brother Mishka, from whom I hear occasionally, in a manner utterly unsuspected by his 'Keepers' in the Zoological Gardens at St. Petersburg, frequently does his best to persuade me to modify my opinion of and conduct towards mankind. He says the humans are not nearly so bad as one thinks, and that he has a very good time in his perpetual berloga (from which the poor fellow cannot escape) and gets plenty of victuals of the best quality. He says he likes children the best – they are so very generous with their buns and cakes. Ha ha! I agree with him about the youngsters! I like the children best, too! They are so deliciously tender and flaky. I have enjoyed several, and sincerely hope I have not tasted my last.

But I must proceed with my narrative. This then was to be the pivot upon which my future career was to turn: hatred of and animosity towards the human race. If I could at any time injure their persons or damage their property it should be done; I had vowed it; that very night as we three children lay huddled and trembling, poor orphans of a murdered mother, within our desolate berloga, we all vowed it. Man was henceforth our enemy.

We were all reduced to great straits just at this time, for a living. Poor little creatures that we were, it puzzles me now, when I think of it, how we managed to pull through that dreadful period. The fact of the matter is, we were obliged to eat all sorts of things which we should otherwise have left alone; it was now April, and we contrived to live upon the young leaves and grass blades and shoots of various trees and bushes, together with – I blush to record it – field-mice, squirrels, an occasional hare, and sometimes a partridge or grey hen, when one could be found obligingly sitting on a nestful of eggs and dreaming of the joys of maternity. We ate the eggs also.

So, we dragged along until July came. But each day life became easier and more enjoyable, for the rye and oats soon began to grow tall in the fields surrounding the villages; the bees were up and about and furnished us with the perfectly delicious results of their labours; and the woods gradually filled themselves with berries and luxuries of all sorts. When the oats were ripe, we fared magnificently.

One day we met a splendid specimen of our family whom we soon discovered to be none other than our father – the consort of our dear mother, now deceased. He received us fairly well; but my veneration for the paternal relative suffered a rude shock when he informed my brother and sister and myself that, with every desire to be a good father to us, he could not permit us to trespass upon a certain oat-field which he declared did not contain any more than he absolutely required for his own subsistence. He made some sympathetic remarks as to mother's death, with his mouth full of delicious ripe oats, and then bade farewell of us (meaning us to go – he evidently had no intention of leaving the field!), remarking, cordially enough, that he would always be glad to see us, and to hear of any favourable feeding-grounds we might come across, if large enough for all, 'but never mind your old father if rations are scarce!' he added. I never saw my parent again.

Very shortly after the day upon which he warned us off that oat-field, which – by the way – we had discovered, he permitted himself to be driven away from its precincts by a mere peasant-human armed with an axe. I fancy my father must be a very inferior person compared with my good brave mother. She would have behaved very differently towards that peasant – we should undoubtedly have had him for supper: oats, peasant, and honey; a supper of three courses fit for the gods. But for a member of the family of Ursidæ to be ignominiously chased away from an oat-field by a peasant – oh! Dear me – disgraceful! disgraceful!

Well, it was a grand time for us, that first summer. How we grew and fattened! By the early part of the autumn, we were really quite respectable-sized members of the community. About this time, we lost our brother Vainka. It was an exciting thing, rather, and I will note down the story in full. It was like this.

We were all three busily engaged in breakfasting among the tall stems of a rye-field, near a village, when we observed several human children playing about in an adjoining belt of pastureland. There were no grown men present, so far as we were aware, and we determined to amuse ourselves, and at the same time to piously observe the injunctions of our dear mother deceased, by doing our best to frighten the brats out of their wits, and, if possible, injure them besides; we were too small, as yet, to do them any very serious harm; in fact, they were rather bigger, I think, than we.

So, we crept towards them, hidden from view by the beautiful thick rye-stalks, until we were close to the edge of the pasture-field. Then, at a signal from Natasha, we all three pounced out upon them, growling and open-mouthed. Oh dear, oh dear! It was a funny sight to see those children! The silly creatures were too startled to move until we were upon them. They stood staring and shrieking, with eyes and mouth open, and turned to run only when it was too late. How we laughed as we rolled them over and over in the grass and scratched their faces and tore their dresses off their backs! And how they screamed!

The whole population of the village rushed out to see what all the noise was about, big men and women with axes and long things called scythes, and then we thought it was time to retire among our rye-stalks. There we hid ourselves and laughed, and ate the delicious cool, juicy grasses, and the luscious rye-grains, until we could eat and laugh no more, and determined to make a move into the woods, in order to have a good drink in a moss pool we knew of and then lie down a bit and sleep off the excitement.

But to our horror we found that those mean wretches, the humans belonging to the village, were waiting for us outside the cover. They had sneaked up and surrounded us, and were sitting silently all along the edge of the field, armed with their axes and scythes and nets; luckily they had no fire-sticks!

Well, Vainka was, as it happened, the first to step out from among the rye-stalks, and he was immediately confronted by two women and a man who ran after him – one getting in front and one on each side. While they were busy with him, however, Natasha and I escaped unnoticed and were able to watch the pursuit of poor Vainka from a position of safety. One of the women had a crawfish net with a long wooden handle. This creature kept calling to the others, 'Don't kill him, don't kill him! we'll take him alive!'

The others seemed to agree, for they closed in upon poor little Vainka and placed the crawfish net tightly over his head and face, so that, though he fought fiercely and bravely for liberty, he was quite powerless to hurt them. Then they led him away to the village and we saw him no more.

I have seen him often since, however, for his 'master' still lives in this village and brings him down from town at certain seasons. Vainka goes to town (St. Petersburg) in order to amuse the people by dancing on his hind legs, pretending to wrestle with his master, and other foolery, and with – I blush to record it – with a ring through his nostrils, to which a chain is attached. Poor dear old Vainka – his spirit is completely broken; he has actually learned to tolerate human-kind and declares that they only require to be known in order to be appreciated, and that he does not think he could exist now without the applause which his performances call forth from the vulgar brutes of humans who have degraded him. Ugh! It is shameful! He has twice escaped from the village and joined me – but I will, I think, relate these episodes in full, in their proper place in this narrative; for my ursine friends may learn much by a careful consideration of the events, and I should not like to deprive them of the advantage of considering this matter in the light of a thorough and intimate knowledge of the circumstances.

Meanwhile, I must relate the sad story of how Natasha and I separated – after, alas, a quarrel. It was after our first winter alone – without mother and the rest, I mean. Natasha and I spent that winter together, in one berloga, for warmth. It was a very uneventful time, for we were not disturbed from November to April, and slept steadily on through all those months. It was then that we realised how dreadfully we must have worried poor dear mother in the preceding year by keeping her awake during that long period when we bears feel as though it were impossible, whatever happened, to rouse ourselves, and would almost sooner die than move.

But to continue: when spring came and we sallied forth from our winter quarters, we were both so hungry that positively we could almost have eaten one another. Just outside a village close by, as we were prowling around, hoping to find some sort of food, Natasha taking one side of the village and I the other, I had made my half round without success and was awaiting my sister with some degree of impatience, when I saw a dog issue from one of the huts and trot away across a field. The next instant I heard a yelping and observed Natasha in full pursuit, and scarcely a yard away from the dog's tail. Then they both disappeared behind a hedge, and for a moment the yelping was redoubled, and then ceased altogether. I hurried along to join and congratulate Natasha, as well as to take my share in a dinner which I felt that I required very badly, when suddenly I met Natasha returning.

'Well, where's the dog?' I said – feeling, I know not why, a strange sinking at the heart.

'What dog?' said Natasha, drooping her head a little and averting her face.

'Why, the dog you were hunting a moment ago!' I said.

'Oh, it escaped,' said Natasha, who had some whitish fur, which was not her own, sticking to the corner of her mouth.

'Oh – you nearly caught it, I see!' said I.

'Yes, I very nearly caught it,' said my sister, her voice dying away to nothing at the end of the sentence.

Well – I believed her, for we had never, as yet, deceived one another to any great extent.

Half an hour afterwards, as we were roaming the woods looking for something solid to eat, I suddenly missed Natasha. I called for her and searched the wood, but all in vain. I therefore left the forest and retraced my steps towards the open fields close, to the village. There, after considerable hunting and much waste of time and temper, I at last came upon my sister, who was just polishing off the last remnants of the carcass of a dog. I fell upon her without a word, for she had deceived me and was unworthy of courtesy at my hands.

Up to this time I had always been polite and kind and – in its best sense – brotherly towards Natasha; therefore, she was astonished and indignant when I attacked her. I must confess I punished her savagely, for I was very angry and very hungry as well; indeed, I did not leave her alone until I had pretty nearly worried the breath out of her body. When she picked herself up from the grass, she made off immediately, without making any remark either of abuse or excuse, and, as I have never set eyes on her since that morning, I conclude that she emigrated to a distant part of the country. I cannot say I was sorry, for I should never have regained that confidence in her which her deceitful conduct on this occasion entirely destroyed, and the relations between us would have been so strained as to render life unpleasant.

So, there was an end of family life for me – as a bachelor, of course. My father – well, the less said about my poor old selfish pater, the better. My mother, bless her, dead; my sister Katia dead also; Mishka and Vainka both prisoners, one at the Zoo, in St. Petersburg, the other in a village not far away from my own domain; and Natasha, as I have explained, an exile – a discredited fugitive from her native woods!

Soon after Natasha's disappearance, however, at least in the autumn of the same year, just before I had chosen the spot in which I should winter, something happened which filled me with true joy and thankfulness: for I have a tender heart in spite of what I have just recorded of my conduct towards Natasha.

I was wandering about the forest feeling very weary, and longing for the first fall of snow to herald in the approaching winter and allow of my retiring for the season. Hearing a noise behind me – a puffing, grunting noise which seemed to indicate the presence of one of my own species, – I turned quickly round to see who this could possibly be; and, if a stranger, to warn him that he was trespassing upon land which already belonged to me by the sacred rights summed up in the ancient Roman law which all bears excepting extremely large ones still recognise as binding: 'beati possidentes [*blessed are the possessors*].' What was my delight to see my dear old brother Vainka puffing and blowing after me as fast as his poor old legs and lungs – both sadly out of condition, – could bring him. He had a ring through his nose, and from this there dangled a piece of chain, and from the end of the chain a torn portion of a halter.

We rushed towards one another:

'Why, Vainka!' I exclaimed: 'where in fortune's name do you come from, and how did you escape?'

'It's a long story!' said Vainka – 'never mind the details – here I am! I bit through the rope, as you see, and escaped from the barn at night by breaking down the door: now let's have some food! When we are in the berloga, which I suppose will be tomorrow – I hope so, for I'm dead tired' (here he yawned twice and I followed suit) – 'I'll tell you all about it.'

I gave him a capital dinner considering the time of year, including some honey – of which I knew of a good store, and showed him the spot I had chosen for the berloga, which he quite approved of.

During the course of conversation, Vainka informed me that he had grown quite fond of his 'master,' and would not care to do him an injury; but at the same time he wished to mention that there were six young sheep grazing in the field behind the house he (Vainka) inhabited, and that he should imagine these sheep would make a delightful meal for any one liking mutton. Personally, he said, he would rather not touch them, and he hoped, for his master's sake, that no one else would; but that they were in such and such a field, and the humans never left the house before 6 a.m. A really good feed, he remarked, was considered by some people to be an advantage just before retiring for a sleep of several months.

He was perfectly right. Those young sheep were quite delicious; and while we gaily consumed them for dinner next day, old Vainka gave me many hints as to the exact disposal, by humans, of their time, – hints which have ever since been extremely useful to me in various ways. Did I mention that Vainka consumed his share of the two sheep which found their way to our larder? Well, he did – anyhow; and enjoyed them very much, but was deeply put out (after he had dined) to remember that the mutton had belonged to his master. He would not, he said, for anything have touched it had he recalled that fact in time.

That day the snow came, and, after performing those maze-like evolutions in which our family invariably indulge at this time of year, and which are designed to bewilder any human being who might wander our way and wish to track us, with sinister purpose, to our lair, we lay down, and overcome by fatigue and – well, mutton – fell asleep almost immediately. I had endeavoured, but in vain, to remove the badge of servitude and disgrace which poor Vainka was condemned to wear in the shape of the ring and chain but could do nothing with it – Vainka had been obliged to settle down with the cruel, detestable thing still attached to his nose – bah!

The next thing either of us was conscious of was a knocking at the sides of our snowy, or icy house. The noise immediately aroused us, for it recalled a similar sound which we had good cause to remember and carried us back to that dreadful day when our poor mother had been done to death, together with little Katia. On peeping through the hole, we soon perceived that we were besieged by two men – both of whom were peasants. One of these held a fire-stick, and the sight of it put my heart all of a quake; for I confess, though I fear nothing else in the world, I am terribly frightened of that dreadful, death-spitting stick, called gun. But Vainka touched my shoulder:

'The one with the gun,' he whispered, 'is my master: what's to be done?'

I didn't know. Then Vainka rose to the emergency and did that for which I shall always feel reverently and admiringly grateful to him. He undertook to see me safely out of the difficulty by giving himself up.

'They'll never dream that you are here as well as I,' he said; 'all you have to do is to stay snugly inside and let me go out: they won't shoot me; I am too valuable to them!'

I protested that this sacrifice was too noble; that I could not permit such self-abnegation on my account!

'Self-abnegation?' said Vainka; 'nonsense! it's nothing of the sort. I declare to you that I would rather go back to the humans than earn my living in the woods; I came away because I pined for the winter sleep for which my nature yearns – I should have had to work, with them; now, I have had my rest and am as fresh as a daisy!'

I really believe the good fellow meant it. At all events, since I should certainly be killed or wounded if I went out and he would as certainly only be captured, it was clearly better that he should go than I; for he might always escape again; while I, if once killed, should appear upon the scene no more. So, I embraced my dear Vainka, thanked him heartily for saving my life at the expense of his liberty (at which he smiled and said he didn't believe in liberty), and let him go – lying very close myself, and watching the development of circumstances through the peephole.

I must say that, in spite of all my hatred for mankind, I was a little softened towards Vainka's friends, on this occasion, by the events which now took place.

Vainka broke through the wall of our berloga and deliberately stepped out. The man with the pole quickly got out of the way, while the other raised his gun. For an instant I was in dread lest he should not recognise my dear brother in time, and was on the point of rushing forth to strike him dead before he should have slaughtered poor confiding Vainka, when, luckily for us all (for I should not have been in time), he dropped his arm, raised his hand to shade his eyes, stared, and broke into a roar of laughter:

'Why!' he cried, 'strike me blind if it isn't dear old Mishka himself!' (The humans, for reasons best known to themselves, call us all 'Mishka.')

With these words, he rushed up to Vainka, caught hold of the chain (the wrench to V.'s nose must have been exceedingly painful!) put both arms round my brother's neck, and commenced to kiss and to hug him in the most comical manner. He really appeared to be quite fond of Vainka, and Vainka himself seemed almost as glad to greet him. Then the peasant took some lumps of the cooked rye, which my brother says is so delicious (and which, I may mention, I believe in my heart to be one of the chief causes of Vainka's marvellous attachment to the debased life he leads!) and fed his newfound and long-lost friend. Vainka dropped a large piece of it on the ground, and I imagine the good fellow meant it for me; but the frugal peasant picked it up and pocketed it, so that I was not able to taste the vaunted stuff – bah! I'm sure it isn't up to July oats or honey, or even baby – which is delicious when one happens to be of a carnivorous turn of mind, as one is sometimes.

Then they all went away and left me, never dreaming – as Vainka rightly anticipated – that another bear lay concealed within the berloga, and that Master Mishka, as they called him, was but my guest. Ha! Ha! I should have liked to have dashed out and smashed them both – the men, I mean, when their backs were turned! I burned to do it – but discretion gained the day: there was that accursed fire-stick to be reckoned with: I have been told that guns can be made to spit their fire in an instant even when a man has been knocked down and is lying upon the ground.

So, I refrained and stayed where I was, and in a while fell asleep once more, sleeping safely and comfortably until April, when I left the den and went out once again upon my travels.

I had one other visit from Vainka, a few months later.

I had been hunting near his village, when of a sudden I became aware of Master V. approaching me through a thin birch spinney which lay between me and the fields around the hamlet. He looked very dejected – not at all as one would expect a bear to look who had just regained his liberty! He brightened up a little when he saw me.

'Is anything the matter, brother?' I inquired, as I went to meet him.

'Nothing whatever,' he said, 'excepting that, curiously enough, I do not feel inclined to escape, and yet here I am, in the act of escaping!'

'But how can that be?' I said; 'in the first place you must be glad to escape – no bear of any self-respect could help feeling glad; and besides, how could you possibly escape against your will?'

'Well,' he said, 'perhaps I have no self-respect; anyhow I only came because they left the door of the stable wide open and my chain was off at the time. All I had to do was to walk out, and now I wish I hadn't! This is just the time when little Masha brings me my lunch of delicious bread' (that's the cooked rye I mentioned), 'and – and – upon my word I think I shall go back – what's the use of being free – I am no longer fitted for a wild life.'

And sure enough, the poor-spirited creature, whose once keen, free spirit had been entirely deadened by contact with the humans and their debasing life, would have made off then and there!

But I stopped him.

'You shall do nothing of the kind, my friend!' I said firmly. 'You shall come into the woods with me and have a good time, and when you've enjoyed a run and some fresh air and natural food, you shall do as you like! Come on!'

So, I got him away, and for three days we had the grandest fun in the world. He cheered up and agreed to join me in a little hunting close to a neighbouring village – he would do nothing near his own. We killed two dogs, a young cow, and some sheep, old Vainka thoroughly entering into the spirit of the fun, and even enjoying the wild fury of the humans, who could not find us – there being no snow.

But after three days of freedom and real life Vainka grew homesick. He yawned frequently and said how sad little Masha would be without him, and wondered what she was doing now – and now, and whether his master – whom, in spite of his solemn vows to our mother, he had evidently learned to love – was quite well – and so on. He became so melancholy and maudlin, that I perceived it was no use fighting against destiny, and I recommended him to be off to his dancing and skipping and his Masha and his confounded man-worship – and away he went – poor fellow! As clear a case of a good bear gone wrong as it has ever been my lot to come across.

The foregoing episode is a narrative of my last visit from Vainka. I have seen the poor old fellow now and again and communicated with him by signs, the nature of which my ursine readers will at once comprehend, but which – in case any artful human should happen to decipher these memoirs – I will not describe in detail. Both Vainka and Mishka are – much as I deplore the fact – now quite gone over to the enemy; they are, both of them, more man than bear, and this in spite of the tragic and bloody reasons which they, in common with myself, should cherish in their deepest hearts for loathing the very creatures whom they have learned to love – bah! It is unnatural, it is unbear-like, it is sickening.

I, for my part, have kept my vow as made to our murdered mother. I think I may fairly boast that this is so. Perhaps if I relate one or two of my principal adventures with mankind, my readers will do me the justice to admit that I have done my best. I hope they will do themselves the justice to follow my example. Mankind should be suppressed, wherever found.

The first human being I successfully attacked and killed was a grown man, a peasant; the second was a baby. The latter was delicious, and I can safely recommend such of my relatives as have adhered, hitherto, to vegetarian principles, to relax them in favour, at least, of this dish.

Babies are not always easily procured; but a little excitement adds, I consider, zest to the pursuit. I may say at once that babies, in spite of the terrible noise which they are undoubtedly capable of producing, are perfectly harmless. They may be found occasionally lying on the grass close to rye or oat fields in which human beings are busy cutting down the food which naturally belongs to us, not to them.

This is an act of burglary, and is punishable with singular propriety; because while these thieving humans are intent upon depriving us of our property it is the easiest matter in the world to creep up and make oneself master of theirs, in the shape of the babies which they leave in the adjoining field, ostensibly to take care of the food and drink which is packed in baskets for their dinner – though I must say it is just like human stupidity to place a helpless thing like a baby in charge of valuable property. I have never yet seen one raise a hand to protect its mother's dinner. But, as usual, I am wandering from my immediate subject, which is – a description of my first man.

It was towards evening one summer day, and I was wandering slowly through the wood. I was not in the best of humours, for a field of oats upon which I had been supporting myself for several days was this afternoon in the hands of the 'reapers,' as they call themselves: thieves, as I call them! I had come there for my dinner and found the gang of humans busy at the oats with scythe and reaping-hook. What could I do? There was nothing to be done, excepting to show my teeth and bristle up my coat at them – and since they did not see me that was not of much practical use! So, I went away again, cross and revengeful, and as I roamed about the woods, fuming and hungry, whom should I meet of a sudden but a tall peasant, wearing an axe in his belt but otherwise unarmed.

For an instant we both stopped, surprised and startled. Then, full of the hatred for his kind which I always felt but which had received an additional stimulus in the oat-field this afternoon, I raised myself upon my hind feet and caught hold of him. He tried to reach his axe, but I had gripped his arm and he could not. His face was a study: he had become very pale, and his eyes were protruding: froth came from his mouth together with spluttering words – bad language, of course; those disgusting peasant creatures never open their lips without using language such as a bear would be shocked to employ.

I leant upon him, bending my whole weight forward, growling fiercely, and reaching for his throat with my teeth. I felt a strong lust for blood, and my rage increased with every second. I knew that I must kill this man, and that he could not escape me or injure me. My fury knew no bounds; I seemed to hate him all the more for being in my power, and I bore him pitilessly down to the earth – I was far heavier than he.

Then I seized his throat in my teeth and his head with my claws and enjoyed myself. How he kicked and struggled for a few seconds – only a few – I wish it had been more! – then he lay perfectly still, and I knew that I had slain my first man. I was not anxious to eat him: I had not as yet learned that human flesh is good, especially that of babies; therefore, I mauled him savagely for several minutes in order to make sure there should be no mistake about his incapacity for future mischief and treachery, which is all that his kind live for – and then I left him to the crows. But as I raised myself from his body, I muttered to myself,

'There, mother! Though thousands of executions could never avenge your assassination, here lies one, at least, of the hated family which murdered you!'

I felt more or less appeased after the pious act of filial vengeance which I have just recorded and ate my supper that night with a light heart – the supper consisting of some of the very oats which the peasants had thought to deprive me of! The silly creatures had cut the oats and tied them in bundles, which was extremely convenient for me, and saved me the trouble of picking the ears of grain for myself.

As for my first baby meal, that was a very simple affair: the small creature was lying, rolling about, in the grass while her mother (I suppose they have mothers, such as they are) was reaping together with a host of other humans in the adjoining field. The forest was the common boundary of the two fields, and all I had to do was to creep a few yards from the wood, take the goods the gods provided, and retire to enjoy them. I did this with entire success, catching hold of the imp with one arm and hobbling along on three feet. But that baby made such a terrific caterwauling that positively I nearly dropped him out of pure anxiety for the drums of my ears.

His mother rushed out from among the oat stalks and ran after me, though she did not see me, in the direction of the baby's cries, but she soon returned: I think one of her companions called to her that it was only the child, was gone and that her dinner was all right, wrapped up in a red pocket handkerchief. Well, that baby was the most delightful thing I had ever tasted, and I then and there determined that this dainty should form an item of my diet whenever obtainable. It is in season all the year round; but difficult to obtain at any time except summer.

I must just add to the above narrative, that as I lay enjoying my dinner within the pine forest, scarcely fifty yards from those peasants, I could distinctly overhear their remarks as to the disappearance of the young human at that moment forming the staple item of my dinner. It appeared that I was not suspected. The whole odium of the affair was laid upon certain people who, however disreputable and disagreeable they may be (and they certainly are both), were at all events innocent of this 'crime.' I mean those impostors and cads, the wolves.

Many of my most successful enterprises in and about villages have been laid to the charge of wolves: so be it! This cannot injure me. True, I should like to have the credit of certain of my exploits! Those in which mankind have been destroyed, especially; but it is very amusing when you have successfully robbed an enemy, to hear someone else blamed and vengeance vowed upon persons who have had nothing whatever to do with the affair.

So it was in the matter of my first baby. Not a man, woman, or child present but endeavoured to console the weeping mother by vowing vengeance upon the thieving 'wolf,' for she really did weep, though, as I have already declared, I did not touch her dinner but only a useless, squealing baby. That she did not really regret the loss of the tiny creature was abundantly proved by her own assertions at the time; for she several times repeated that it was, after all, 'better so;' that the baby would never be hungry again (that it certainly would not!), or feel pain or worry of any sort, with more to the same effect, and all, of course, perfectly true. For all that, she cried steadily on, as she worked, and many of the other women cried also, though they all agreed as to the fact that things were better as they were and repeated this a hundred times. Of course, things were better as they were.

What better or worthier thing could a human baby do than provide a dinner for one of the Ursidæ? All I desired was that they should so thoroughly feel the force of the truism, as to bring me another tender morsel without delay. This, however, they did not do. On the contrary, they brought dogs instead of babies, and I felt that, though dog is tasty enough when nothing better is obtainable, I would transfer my custom, for the present, to another parish.

And now I propose to dismiss for a while the disagreeable subject of the human race, and to give my readers a glimpse into some of the dangers and difficulties which I have at different times of my life encountered while living the free and, on the whole, happy life of the woods.

I have incidentally referred to certain persons for whom I have the supremest contempt, as for animals of an altogether inferior rank in the scale of life: that is, inferior to our own; I would not go so far as to say that they are not superior to humans, for the latter, when without their detestable fire-sticks, are contemptibly weak and defenceless: their teeth are ridiculously inefficient, and as for their claws – well, they have none, so far as I can ascertain. The creatures I refer to are wolves, as they call themselves.

These are the very plebeians of the forest. They are hated by every resident, great or small; for they are mean and cowardly creatures, hunting in companies of three or four – they dare not show themselves singly – and sometimes in packs of a dozen or more. A wolf, if unaccompanied by his friends, would probably run away from a hare, and hide himself from a little red fox. They are thieves of the first water, besides, and have no respect whatever for the rights of property. Many a time have I left a portion of some choice repast which I was not capable of consuming at one sitting, expecting to find and enjoy the remains on the following night. What I actually found was a few white bones and the vision of two grey tails stuffed tightly between four hind legs just in the act of disappearing into the cover – ugh! They are cads – cads, that is just the word, the only word for them.

Well, one fine evening, about September a year or two ago, as I was strolling through the wood thinking of – well, I'll tell you all about that presently – enough that I was thinking of someone and feeling rather love-sick and depressed – when I suddenly heard a cantering noise behind me, and turning round I beheld seven very large wolves coming up on my scent. The instant that I turned round the whole party stopped, sat down on their haunches, and stared at me.

They looked hungry and wicked but would not meet my eye. I darted at the nearest, but in a moment he and his companions had disappeared – in the marvellous way which these cowards understand so well. Oh ho! I thought, if you are afraid to stand up to me you will certainly not dare to pursue me! So, I made off towards that portion of the forest in which I generally took my night's rest. But I was mistaken in my conclusions, for no sooner was I well on my way, than the cantering sound recommenced, and the wolves were after me again. It was useless to stop and attack them, for they are too active to be caught in this way; I therefore decided to push along and take no notice.

But before many minutes had elapsed, the leading wolf began to set up that loathsome howling of theirs and was immediately imitated by the rest. I hate noise, so I hurried on, hoping to shake them off – for I had not as yet realised that these plebeians were actually organising a pursuit with the ultimate object of tiring me out and pulling me down.

After all it takes some little while for the very idea of such an unexampled insult as this to take root in the patrician mind: me to be pursued and pulled down by wolves! The thing was outrageous, impossible! But I confess I was somewhat disconcerted when I realised that the wolves were howling with a purpose; for in a very few minutes I was aware of new arrivals among my pursuers: grey forms with bright, hungry eyes, appeared in the moonlight to right and left of me; one or two cantered on ahead – it was really growing a little exciting.

I stopped once more and turned to survey the pack and count the new arrivals. As if by magic, each wolf stopped dead and sat down, some concealing themselves behind trees, others looking away; none ventured to assume a threatening aspect as far as I could ascertain there were now nearly twenty wolves present: the situation was not altogether a pleasant one. Then I played a successful little ruse upon them. I turned as though to fly, taking a few rapid strides forward; then I suddenly stopped, and, as I had expected, the leader shot up to my side before he could control the impetus which he had already gained.

Well – I had him in a moment, and I have reason to believe his own mother would not have recognised him a minute or two afterwards, for I made a very complete wreck of him, and left him literally torn to pieces. During the operation, which did not occupy me very long, his companions had totally disappeared: there was neither sound nor sight of them. But shall I be believed? No sooner did I leave him and continue my journey than the unnatural creatures, instantly reappearing from every side, fell upon their mangled brother and consumed his body, quarrelling and snarling and fighting over him like so many devils, which I believe they are under an assumed name!

I thought, for a while, that I had shaken off the thieving brutes, but this was not the case. I soon found that they were after me once more, howling and snarling, every devil's son of them! I own that at this point I suddenly lost heart and, to use a familiar expression, took to my heels. I make this confession in all humility and with shame. Why I lost heart I cannot explain. I have mentioned the depression of spirits from which I was suffering this night, and I can only suppose that it was the pandemonium of noise made by my pursuers which, acting upon a state of mind already somewhat enfeebled by the depression referred to, had relaxed my nerve-power and caused me to disgrace myself in the manner indicated.

So I fled, I own it with shame; I fled at the top of my speed, pursued by the howling pack of miserable plebs, which dared not come very close, but followed me some ten yards behind and at each side, trusting to my bulk and weight, which they hoped would prove so cumbrous that I should be unable to run far without collapsing into a defenceless condition of breathlessness and weakness, when they would, they imagined, pull me down.

Well, so far as the breathlessness was concerned, they proved perfectly right. Not being accustomed to much running, I was naturally out of condition; and consequently, before I had run many miles I felt that this sort of thing could not continue: I must devise some scheme by which to put to flight or to evade the enemy. Then this idea suddenly struck me: Why not climb a tree? Wolves are notoriously incapable of climbing (after all, what can a wolf do?). I should thus at least gain time enough to recover my breath and consider my position.

No sooner thought of than done. I had not enjoyed much climbing of late, so that I anticipated some little trouble and exertion in reaching the required altitude; therefore, I pushed along until I saw a tree which looked easy to climb; then I ran to its foot, stopped, and turned round.

As before, the wolves instantly, paused and sat down; while some, as usual, disappeared. I immediately commenced the ascent of my tree refuge. But no sooner did the wolves realise that this was my intention than they seemed to gather courage from the prospect of losing me, and with redoubled howls and noise they surrounded the tree and actually dared to grab at my hind legs as I swarmed up the trunk. I sustained one or two nasty bites during that degrading moment, but those bites did for me what perhaps nothing else would have done.

They restored me to myself, and in addition inspired me with so terrible and righteous a fury (and when we bears do lose our tempers we certainly are properly angry!) that in an instant I was down and among my pursuers – tearing, hugging, crushing! – oh, when I remember that triumphant moment of crushing bones and ripping flesh my heart fills with the emotion of pride and thankfulness to reflect that I was born a bear and no other meaner creature! True, I have never seen a lion, or tiger – both of which animals, tradition says, are capable of slaying a bear; but with all deference to tradition, I prefer to think otherwise. I am told that lions and tigers are both cats – cats! I have seen, and I may add eaten, many cats, and howsoever large and fierce these traditional members of the family may be, I beg leave to state that, speaking for the Ursidæ generally, we shall be delighted to see any number of lions, or tigers, or any other form of cats in these parts, and to try conclusions with them. My brother Mishka has seen, in the distance, specimens of the creatures referred to in his home at the Zoological Gardens, and does not think much of them, though, he says, they are large. Well, size is nothing; a cow is big enough, in all conscience, but I have never had the slightest difficulty in negotiating a cow, however large.

But to continue: it was a real pleasure to me – though I have seldom been so angry – to rend and crush those too enterprising wolves who had presumed to attack my person. When I had done with them, three lay stiff and stark, while two others were limping and howling somewhere out of sight among the bushes.

As for me, I had a scratch or two, but nothing to matter. I need hardly say that I was not molested again as I deliberately climbed that tree and settled myself for the rest of the night in a cosy corner among the branches. But no sooner was I out of their reach than a dozen wolves came howling around the trunk and leaping up in pretended anxiety to get at me. They were but playing a part in order to deceive one another, of course; but this is the way of wolves, who have no dignity and self-respect. Had I shown so much as one tooth they would have instantly disappeared!

So, the night passed away, in perfect comfort for me and with quite as much actual repose as could be expected, having regard to the pandemonium going on below, where the wolves quarrelled and fought over the bodies of their relatives, entirely consuming them among themselves in a wonderfully short space of time. I was much amused to watch their dealings with the wounded heroes who turned up to claim a share in the feast. Not being in a condition to fight for the disgusting food, they were themselves promptly set upon, slain by their unwounded brethren, and eaten with the greatest gusto.

Whether my besiegers were satiated with the feast I had thus provided for them, or whether – like all malefactors – they were afraid of the daylight, I know not; but it is certain that soon after the last bone had been picked, and just as the sun began to show signs in the east of his intentions with regard to another day, they all departed. Had they remained, I should have attacked them presently; and they would have run like sheep!

Wolves, as I have already remarked, are dreadful cowards. I shall scarcely be believed, perhaps, but it is a positive fact, that I have seen three of them sitting in the snow around a dying man who was unarmed and perfectly helpless, waiting until he should have breathed his last breath before they dared pounce upon him. I came upon the party accidentally.

The man had lost himself in the snow and was slowly dying of fatigue and cold and hunger. It was rather amusing, for it must have been a considerable trial to him to have those wolves sitting there, and to know that they did but await his death or stupor. Now, I had no great desire to eat that man: I don't care much for tough, grown-up humans; but I gave him a touch sufficient to knock the breath out of his body and ate him all the same. I always take the opportunity to pay off old scores; and here was a double one.

However, taking one thing with another, I am really not quite sure that I do not dislike wolves even more than men: I certainly despise them more. A man will, as a rule, stand up to an enemy, even to a superior creature like myself; whereas a wolf will never fight until he is wounded so badly that he cannot run away. Since my little adventure with the pack of wolves, I have never felt the slightest vestige of respect for their class. I cannot forget the sickening spectacle of those cowardly humbugs jumping up around the tree in which I sat, as though they were anxious to get at me – bah!

But there! I must not allow my tongue to wag any longer; I am getting old, I suppose, and garrulous, but I do love to fight over again those countless battles with my enemies, which have made of me the far-renowned champion that I am. Up to now my teeth are as sharp, my arms as powerful, and my heart as sound as in the days of my youth; but there will come a time, I suppose, when teeth and claws will become blunt, and sight dim; when a grouse rising suddenly from the thicket will startle me, and a hare crossing my path will make my heart to beat – ah, well! When that time arrives, may the end come soon, for I could never bear to support a feeble existence!

When I feel that I am no longer a match for my enemies, I am determined what to do: I shall seek out a human who is armed. With his fire-stick, he shall free my soul from my body; but with my last strength I shall grip his throat and tear his life from him, so that our two souls shall journey together to those happy hunting-grounds where we are to handle the fire-weapon, and the men to do the running: I shall like to have a human soul handy to start upon as soon as I arrive in those blessed regions; and oh! If I happen to meet my dear mother, how she will enjoy taking a share in the hunt!

However, I am all right here for the present, and life is pleasant enough while one's teeth are sharp!

From: The Romance of the Woods

The Great Flood

ONCE UPON A time, there was a widow who had a child. And the child was a kind-hearted boy of whom everyone was fond.

One day he said to his mother: 'All the other children have a grandmother, but I have none. And that makes me feel very sad!'

'We will hunt up a grandmother for you,' said his mother. Now it once happened that an old beggar-woman came to the house, who was very old and feeble. And when the child saw her, he said to her: 'You shall be my grandmother!'

And he went to his mother and said: 'There is a beggar-woman outside, whom I want for my grandmother!'

And his mother was willing and called her into the house; though the old woman was very dirty. So, the boy said to his mother: 'Come, let us wash Grandmother!'

And they washed the woman. But she had a great many burrs in her hair, so they picked them all out and put them in a jar, and they filled the whole jar.

Then the grandmother said: 'Do not throw them away, but bury them in the garden. And you must not dig them up again before the great flood comes.'

'When is the great flood coming?' asked the boy.

'When the eyes of the two stone lions in front of the prison grow red, then the great flood will come,' said the grandmother.

So the boy went to look at the lions, but their eyes were not yet red. And the grandmother also said to him: 'Make a little wooden ship and keep it in a little box.'

And this the boy did. And he ran to the prison every day and looked at the lions, much to the astonishment of the people in the street.

One day, as he passed the chicken-butcher's shop, the butcher asked him why he was always running to the lions.

And the boy said: 'When the lions' eyes grow red then the great flood will come.'

But the butcher laughed at him. And the following morning, quite early, he took some chicken-blood and rubbed it on the lions' eyes. When the boy saw that the lions' eyes were red, he ran swiftly home, and told his mother and grandmother.

And then his grandmother said: 'Dig up the jar quickly and take the little ship out of its box.'

And when they dug up the jar, it was filled with the purest pearls and the little ship grew larger and larger, like a real ship.

Then the grandmother said: 'Take the jar with you and get into the ship. And when the great flood comes, then you may save all the animals that are driven into it; but human beings, with their black heads, you are not to save.'

So, they climbed into the ship, and the grandmother suddenly disappeared.

Now it began to rain, and the rain kept falling more and more heavily from the heavens. Finally, there were no longer any single drops falling, but just one big sheet of water which flooded everything.

Then a dog came drifting along, and they saved him in their ship. Soon after came a pair of mice, with their little ones, loudly squeaking in their fear. And these they also saved. The water was already rising to the roofs of the houses, and on one roof stood a cat, arching her back and mewing pitifully. They took the cat into the ship, too. Yet the flood increased and rose to the tops of the trees. And in one tree sat a raven, beating his wings and cawing loudly. And him, too, they took in. Finally, a swarm of bees came flying their way. The little creatures were quite wet and could hardly fly. So, they took in the bees on their ship. At last, a man with black hair floated by on the waves.

The boy said: 'Mother, let us save him, too!'

But the mother did not want to do so. 'Did not Grandmother tell us that we must save no black-headed human beings?'

But the boy answered: 'We will save the man in spite of that. I feel sorry for him and cannot bear to see him drifting along in the water.'

So, they also saved the man.

Gradually the water subsided. Then they got out of their ship and parted from the man and the beasts. And the ship grew small again and they put it away in its box.

But the man was filled with a desire for the pearls. He went to the judge and entered a complaint against the boy and his mother, and they were both thrown into jail. Then the mice came and dug a hole in the wall. And the dog came through the hole and brought them meat, and the cat brought them bread, so they did not have to hunger in their prison.

But the raven flew off and returned with a letter for the judge. The letter had been written by a god, and it said: 'I wandered about in the world of men disguised as a beggar woman. And this boy and his mother took me in. The boy treated me like his own grandmother and did not shrink from washing me when I was dirty. Because of this, I saved them out of the great flood by means of which I destroyed the sinful city wherein they dwelt. Do you, O judge, free them, or misfortune shall be your portion!'

So, the judge had them brought before him, and asked what they had done, and how they had made their way through the flood. Then they told him everything, and what they said agreed with the god's letter. So, the judge punished their accuser, and set them both at liberty.

When the boy had grown up, he came to a city of many people, and it was said that the princess intended to take a husband. But in order to find the right man, she had veiled herself, and seated herself in a litter, and she had had the litter, together with many others, carried into the marketplace. In every litter sat a veiled woman, and the princess was in their midst. And whoever hit upon the right litter, he was to get the princess for his bride. So, the youth went there, too, and when he reached the marketplace, he saw the bees whom he had saved from the great flood, all swarming about a certain litter. Up he stepped to it, and sure enough, the princess was sitting in it. And then their wedding was celebrated, and they lived happily ever afterward.

From: The Chinese Fairy Book

Finis

Workbooks From The Scheherazade Foundation

We hope that you have enjoyed this collection of stories, gleaned from varying cultural corners of the world, and that you have been entertained by them.

But, have you considered the deeper meanings and interwoven layers that lie hidden beneath the surface?

At The Scheherazade Foundation, we believe that Teaching-Stories contain wisdom, information, and marvels that have the power to transform the way we think, and thereby change our lives.

Employed as a bedrock of culture throughout the centuries – challenging established patterns of thinking, while passing on knowledge and values – tales such as the ones contained in this volume are a rich resource ready and waiting to be mined.

As an aid to help in the perception of less-obvious facets and layers, we have created a series of original Workbooks. Aimed at stimulating thought-provoking discussions and igniting deep reflection, these tools will assist in unlocking the power of Teaching-Stories.